SUNRISE AT PELICAN BEACH

BOOK FIVE

MICHELE GILCREST

PAYTON

My ankles were swollen and my body felt like it was taking on the shape of a baby elephant. At less than a month away from my due date, the twins were growing limited on space and using their momma's belly as a serious punching bag. My wedding ring barely fit over my knuckle and I was waddling like a duck, but unless the doctor imposed strict orders, I was going to be present at my photography store, and there was nothing anyone could say to change my mind. Thankfully, my sister, Abby, was working by my side and pulling a lot of the weight. To make matters worse, the air conditioning in the store was on the blink. With the Florida heat and sweat beads rolling down my back, I propped up on a stool behind the counter and fanned myself while waiting for our repair guy to show.

"Would you like some ice water to help keep you cool, Payton?" Abby asked.

"Yes, please. I'll take that plus a bucket full to dowse all over myself. Do you remember when we were kids how we used to chase Rebecca with the hose to help cool off?"

"Do I? It wasn't summer unless there was some sort of outdoor water fight involved. Shoot, we used to beg mom and dad to bring out the hose and the kiddie pool every year around April." Abby recalled.

"I don't remember the exact time, but I know we started early. By the time we moved to the beach, it was a wrap. Mom used to say we were natural born water babies. I think she was right."

A bolt of lightning zipped through the sky, and dark grey clouds made it look like nightfall outside. I caught a glimpse of the new owner of the store across the street making his best attempt to unload his moving truck, but the rapidly approaching storm was threatening to bring everything to a screeching halt.

"Hey, Abby, did I mention to you I heard from my assistant, Natalie, over the weekend?" I asked.

"No, how's she doing? Did she say anything about when she's returning to the store?"

"She's doing okay, but as suspected, she decided to make a new home with her aunt in Texas. I can't blame her, really. She was great about checking in every couple of months, but I could always detect the sound of doubt in her voice whenever I said anything about her return. To be honest, I think she's better off. What's a teenager to do after losing her mother? It's not like she had any other family members here in Pelican Beach," I said, feeling sad at the thought of her being alone.

"You have a good point there."

"Abby, I know you took over Natalie's role to help until she returned. I mean, back then the timing couldn't have been more perfect. You were hunting for a job to help Wyatt with the bills, and Lord knows, I needed help fast. But, I was wondering... now that Natalie is not returning, how would you feel about having a more permanent position? You know, making Picture Perfect your permanent gig," I asked.

Abby thought for a moment before a slow smile started emerging.

"You mean, permanent as in, I don't have to worry about having to start the job hunt all over again? And, permanent as in I can still work around the kids pick up and drop off schedule for school?" Abby asked.

"That's exactly what I mean. I can't think of a better fit for the job. You already know this business as well as I do, and we've never been at odds while working together. I think the experience has brought us closer. If you'll agree to it, then the job is yours to keep. Of course, I'll continue to interview for part-time help while I'm out on maternity leave, so the load wouldn't become overbearing. This time I think hiring a photographer would make the most sense. But overall, what do you think?"

"I'm grateful for the opportunity. I don't know what to say. Do you know how hard it is to come by a job with flexible hours for moms with young kids? Especially for someone like myself who hasn't worked in ages. If you would've asked me a few years ago, I would've thought you were insane. Being home with the kids has always been my number one priority. But, Wyatt and I have a way to go before we climb ourselves out of this mountain of debt we're in. So, my answer without a shadow of a doubt is yes, yes, and more yes. Thank you so much." Abby hugged me from behind, practically choking me around the neck.

I loved my sister, but with all the heat, sweat, and extra layer of weight I was carrying, I was inclined to settle for a high five and more ice water.

"You're welcome, sis. Glad to have you," I responded.

"Not to change the subject, but have you met the new owner across the street yet?" Abby asked as she pulled up our website on her computer screen.

"Not yet. Word around town is he just moved here from Jersey. He's into clock repairs, I think. I've seen him coming back and forth by himself with no sign of a wife and kids yet. He's way too good looking to be single, but if he is, he doesn't know what he's in for in this beach town. I can think of a few that will be ready to eat him alive. The women of Pelican Beach don't mess around with finding a good catch," I said, jokingly, even though there was some truth to it.

"Ugh, I'm glad we're married and way past that stage. If I had to start all over again, I don't know what I'd do with myself. Getting out there and making yourself vulnerable...I just can't imagine," Abby said.

"Oh, you'd manage just fine. Look at me. If I'm not a product of starting over and making it through to the other side, then I don't know who is. I survived and you would too if it came down to it."

"You are one of the strongest women I know," she said.

"You... me...Rebecca...mom. Being strong is in our blood. Our battles may look slightly different, but we're all a tough bunch if you ask me."

Another flash of lightning zipped through the sky. The rolling thunder that followed made the glass countertop vibrate.

"Gosh. How long is this supposed to keep up? At this rate

we're going to have a pretty slow afternoon. You better turn on the radio and listen for a storm watch or tornado warnings," Abby said while looking outside.

"Great. That's all I need. Imagine me waddling down to the basement for shelter. Listen, at this rate I'm less worried about the storm and more concerned about us spending another day with a broken down AC unit. I don't know how you can deal with it, to be honest," I said, shaking my head in disgust.

I was already putting up with a lot of non-negotiable things that went along with pregnancy. But no air conditioning... in June... in Florida? That was simply out of the question.

The lights flickered off and on for a few minutes before completely going out. We looked at each other and shrieked at another loud clap of thunder.

"Somehow I highly doubt the repair guy is coming before this storm lets up. Do you have any spare flashlights to help me see my way around the back room?" Abby asked.

I pulled open a drawer and shuffled a few things around. My one and only flashlight was filled with corroded batteries.

"I'm afraid we're out of luck. This flashlight is useless," I said.

"Not a problem. We need a few battery operated lights if I'm going to get anything accomplished before noon. It's dark in here. If I make a run for it, I can zip down to the general store and be back in no time."

"But, Abby, you'll get soaking wet. Why don't you wait it out a bit? The lights will probably come back on in a little while," I said.

"And if they don't? How quickly you forget... we lost power for nearly two hours the last time we had a storm like this.

Thankfully, we were home, but still. I'm not taking any chances. The general store will have everything we need, and I'll be back in no time."

"All right. Take my poncho with you and be careful," I said.

"Careful? I'm just going down the street. What do you think I'm going to do? Get struck by lightning?" Abby teased.

"No, wise guy. I'm just looking out for my big sis, that's all. This storm is mighty wicked."

Abby offered a few additional words of comfort before pulling my poncho over her head and dashing out into the rain. I shook my head, thinking about her strong will and determination before returning to my junk drawer, sifting through with very little daylight. I pulled out a few business cards, a hairbrush, and some old paperwork when I heard the bells to the front door jingle.

"Hi, welcome to Picture Perfect," I said while turning around.

A woman stood there, about 5'6, drenched, with dark curls dripping down her face. She wore red lipstick, a sopping wet sundress, and stood barefoot holding her sandals. While panting heavily she said, "Hi, I'm looking for the owner, Payton."

This woman was breathing so hard you would've thought someone was chasing after her. It gave me an unnerving feeling, but I assumed it was the storm that chased her in.

"I'm Payton. Can I help you?"

She gave me the once over from my face, past my pregnant belly, and even stared at what I presumed was my wedding rings for a moment.

"Ma'am?" I said.

"Yes, you can. My name is Maxine." She extended her hand across the counter.

"Maxine Waters." She continued.

The name sounded vaguely familiar. Before I had enough time to process where I may have heard it, she asked for a few paper towels to dry off with.

"Uh, sure. Here's a roll of paper towels. I wish I had a beach towel to offer but unfortunately, I never usually bring that sort of thing to the store," I said.

"No problem. This will do, thanks," she said.

She patted her face dry, revealing raccoon eyes from her running mascara. The name Maxine danced around in my mind and baffled the heck out of me. I blamed it on my pregnancy brain. I couldn't seem to remember anything as of late.

"Have we met before?" I asked.

"No, not really. We've never officially met, but I sent you a letter a while back. One I was hoping to get a response to, but..." Her voice trailed off.

Immediately it hit me. This was Maxine Waters, the woman who was marrying my ex-husband, Jack. The lame, cheating, low-life who served me divorce papers years ago, but who never seemed to truly disappear out of my life. In one way or another, he always slithered back. This moment was no exception.

I rested my hand on my hip.

"Yes, Maxine. To what do I owe this pleasure?" I asked.

"I was hoping we could talk. I know this is your place of business, but I'm in town for a couple of weeks. Jack's here for a conference. We extended our stay to enjoy a mini vacation after he's finished with work."

I delivered half a smile with an expression that hopefully conveyed *I could not care less.*

"You're right, it is my place of business, and I'm not interested in getting involved," I said.

"Payton, I won't take much of your time. I've just been through so much with Jack. With the wedding coming and all, I know it's not ideal for you to talk to someone like me. I'm the new woman, I get it. But, I can't think of anyone who can understand what I've been going through better than you."

Maxine held her head down in shame.

"I'm hesitant about moving forward with the wedding. Having a conversation with someone who knows him the way I do could make all the difference, Payton," she pleaded.

"Maxine, you and Jack have to sift through your own problems. I stopped being a part of his life a long time ago, and I'm not about to get involved now just because you're having a little cold feet."

The bells on the front door rang. Abby emerged, soaking wet, while rambling about the weather outside.

"Ugh, Payton, you will not believe I ran out of here and left my wallet. I got to the general store and made it halfway down aisle five before realizing I didn't have any money on me," she said.

I glanced over at Abby briefly and then glared at Maxine, hoping she would retreat and leave.

"Payton, is everything okay?" Abby asked.

While continuing to stare at Maxine, I responded.

"Couldn't be better. This lady mistakenly thought she was in the right place. She was just making her way to the front door before you came in."

Abby looked puzzled by the tone in my voice but didn't

question me. Maxine stood on the other side of the counter for another moment. Then she reached inside her bag and laid down a business card with writing on the back.

"Here's my number in case you change your mind," she said.

Then she lowered her voice almost to the point of sounding desperate.

"I understand why you don't want to talk to me. I really do. But, please, Payton. If there's any part of you that can relate to that gut wrenching feeling when you fear your man is cheating. If there's any part of you that remembers that feeling... the awful heartache and torment of needing to know, then I beg of you to call me so we can talk further," Maxine said.

She tucked her hair behind her ear and walked out of the store. I stood frozen in complete disbelief.

JOLENE

$\mathcal{I}$ kept David company and unloaded all the troubles that were festering in my mind as he slid me another glass of brandy. At least two or three times a week I hung out at the bar at the inn to get out of the house and clear my head. Taking care of my cousin Will and catering to his wife, Helen, had been both a blessing and a curse, and at times I needed to vent. David had become my sounding board. He was more than just the new owner of the former family business at the inn, he was my voice of reason and my friend.

"Jolene, I'm assuming you have a lot on your mind tonight if you're working on your third glass. You ready to open up and tell me what's going on? Or do you need me to pry it out of you?" he asked.

"Eh, it's the usual. Will is growing increasingly quiet with the dementia and when he does speak, he normally mutters about something that happened ages ago. Sometimes he doesn't recognize me at all. He just looks straight through me as if he's seen a ghost. Other times he calls me by name. Helen, on the other hand, is growing increasingly bossy. When we're getting along it's great, but she has her expectations about how I ought to live under her roof, and I just don't think I have what it takes to deal with it, anymore. As I said, it's the usual."

"Jolene, I've been gone for what- almost three weeks now? You mean to tell me you haven't pulled Helen aside and asked her to have a talk about what's bothering you by now?" he asked.

"Why should I? It's not like my views will be respected. It's their house and she expects me to play by her rules. *Jolene, why are you playing those records so loud? Jolene, haven't you had enough to drink, dear? Jolene this and Jolene that.* Ugh. Half the time I walk around with headphones plugged in just to hear something other than my name being called repeatedly for no good reason." I complained.

"You are just as much to blame for not saying something, Jolene. Just because you work for them as a private nurse, and just because they're your family members, doesn't mean you don't deserve your privacy and some downtime," David said as he wiped down the bar.

"That's just it. Working for family isn't for everybody. When I first came here, I needed a fresh start. Or at least I thought I did. I had the overwhelming responsibility of taking care of the house that my husband George and I had together. The place needed a lot of repairs, and the bills just kept coming. Plus, I was lonely. I needed relief, so I came here to Pelican Beach in search of a new beginning. I figured taking care of Will would be great if it meant they could avoid putting him in a nursing home-"

"And you envisioned yourself having a life of your own

when you weren't working. Didn't you? Only problem is that doesn't exist. You're always on the clock, Jolene, and now you're getting sick and tired of it. I can hear it in your voice," he said.

I processed everything David was saying, and it was true. I was chasing this vision of how I wanted my life to be, but I was far from living the dream.

"I guess you would know a lot about living out your dreams, wouldn't you? I mean just look at you. You own multiple inns, pick up and travel on a whim, and you're happy. You don't have a care in the world, do you, David?" I asked.

"Well, I wouldn't say that."

He whipped the dishtowel over his shoulder and stood with his arms folded.

"I don't think I'm too far off, David. You are living out your dream to the fullest and you know it."

"Yeah, but I live a pretty lonely life."

"That's by design. You always told me you'd rather be alone. You said something about it, giving you the time needed to focus on your businesses. If I know right, you're probably a ladies' man, anyway. I see the way these women look at you around here." I laughed.

"Ha! A ladies' man? Where on earth did you get that idea? The only lady I spend any amount of time with is you, sitting right here at this bar whenever I'm in town."

"Oh, please, I'm not talking about me. I'm at least seven or eight years older than you. I'm talking about one of these young ladies around here that like to gawk and drool all over you in that cowboy hat of yours. Don't deny it, I know you have a few of them stashed away somewhere."

David leaned over the bar and looked me straight in the eye.

"I'm not a ladies' man, Jolene. I'm an honorable man who knows how to treat a woman right."

He gently removed my glass with the small remainder of brandy in it and poured it in the sink. I didn't know whether to be offended that I didn't get to finish my drink or what. But something about it felt like he was being protective, so I let it go.

"Come on, don't go getting all sensitive on me. I was just messing around with you, David. It's just strange to see a guy like yourself single and successful without a lady by your side. I'm sure guys like yourself have to do something to keep warm at night," I said.

"Yeah, well, just know that it's not by choice that I'm alone. A lot about me has changed over the last year. I'm not opposed to settling down in a relationship. It's getting to be more challenging with each passing year to keep up with having businesses in different states. The staff is amazing and all, but I can't keep up this pace forever. I notice the couples that come here and stay at the inn. Some older, some younger, laughing, walking arm in arm, enjoying their lives together. I just haven't settled down long enough to do anything about it," he said.

"Well, that settles it then. You and I both have some changes to make in our lives and I can't think of a better time to start than now. What do you say we come up with a plan, set a deadline, and follow through on whatever it is we set out to do?"

"It's not that simple in my case but it sounds doable for you," David responded.

"I don't see why you can't take part. Take baby steps. You

say you want to settle down, so why don't you put your feelers out there for a buyer for your other locations?"

"Okay, and what about you?" he asked.

"Oh, I'll need a little more time and perhaps another glass of brandy to help me mull over it a bit more. I'll come up with something. You wait and see."

David came around from behind the bar and positioned himself in between me and the bar stool next to me. His cologne had a manly firewood scent, and his thick gray beard was neatly trimmed.

"Jolene, the brandy is just a band-aid covering up all the areas that hurt, but it's not allowing you to heal. What you really need can't be found in that glass. I think you already know that, don't you?" David asked.

I was fidgeting with a little handkerchief that I kept in my pocket. David was right, but the brandy soothed me. It warmed me up in some ways, but made me numb to being a widow for many years, losing my home, and numb to the unrest with the way I was currently living my life. But now I wanted more. I wanted to go home, back to Jacksonville, where I belonged.

"Your silence tells me I'm right. So, the assignment I have for you tonight is to go home and consider what you're going to say when you talk to your family. Then allow yourself to dream again. Dream of all the fun things you planned on doing when you were moving here to Pelican Beach. I want to see you back here at the inn on Sunday evening, but not here at the bar. Meet me over at the Veranda at seven," he said.

"What's happening at the Veranda?"

"You'll see. Just be there at seven."

David tapped the back of my chair and walked off to greet some of his customers.

I couldn't quite figure him out, but I know one thing was for certain. He was right. I needed to come up with a plan to approach the topic of leaving when I spoke to Helen. I also needed to dream and make a plan for living my best life back home in Jacksonville.

PAYTON

On the first Sunday of the month, the ladies gathered at the beach to catch up over lunch. My sisters Abby and Rebecca were in charge of bringing the food, my mother-in-law, Alice, brought the beverages, and mom and I covered the desserts. Cousin Jolene stayed at the cottage to look after dad.

"As many times as we've reworked the schedule for our gatherings, I think the first Sunday of the month is a perfect fit, don't you?" I asked.

"Sunday works for me. I love that we're finally back into a routine of getting together. Sometimes we're just too busy for our own good," Mom responded.

"You can say that again. The schedule is only going to get worse once the twins arrive. Isn't that right, Payton?" Rebecca said.

"That's what everyone else seems to think. I expect that I'll need time to recover from the c-section, and I'm sure having babies around the house will be quite a change. But, I say as soon as they're old enough, I don't see why we can't bring them out here and get used to beach life. We can set up an umbrella and let the sound of the ocean waves lull them to sleep," I said.

"You say that now, Payton, but once the babies arrive, they're the ones who will dictate where you're going and how long you get to stay," Abby said.

Alice and mom nodded in agreement.

"Trust your sister, Payton. Being a step-mother to a pre-teen is completely different from being a mother to infants. I would imagine by the time the twins arrive we'll be bringing Sunday lunch over to your place," Alice said.

I sat listening to the ladies carry on about just how much my life was about to change over a bowl of tortilla chips and salsa. I'll give them credit for having the experience, but I was still determined to make it work.

"It's just nice to have the husbands keep the kids at least one day out of the month. That way we can pretend to be care-free, if only for a few hours," Abby said while drawing her hair in a bun and stretching out on her beach towel.

"Agreed. On another note, I was thinking it might be nice if we could have a family gathering toward the end of the summer. It would give everyone a chance to meet the twins, plus we could invite some of our cousins that we haven't seen in ages. What do you think?" I asked.

"It would be nice, but it certainly would take a lot of planning. After throwing your baby shower last month, I don't think I have an ounce of planning left in me," Rebecca said.

"You wouldn't have to do it alone. We'd all pitch in. I think it's a great idea. We could host it right here at the cottage. I'll recruit Jolene's help with planning the logistics, and Alice, you're more than welcome to invite your side of the family as well. It can be one big family affair," Mom said.

"It sounds like a lot of fun," Alice replied.

It was fitting for us to be planning a summer gathering. Gathering is what we're good at. Birthdays, Fourth of July celebrations, engagements, weddings, you name it. The only person who may need a little more coaxing to get on board with the idea was Cousin Jolene.

"I thought it might be a good idea to encourage Jolene to invite a few people as well. I don't know about y'all, but she doesn't seem very happy lately," I said.

"Oh, what else is new? Jolene was born grouchy. I wouldn't worry about it too much. I'll let her know she can invite a few people and that should cheer her up," Mom replied.

I didn't want to pry, but from what I could tell, mom and cousin Jolene were everything but fine. Their usual spats had increased, Jolene was spending more time out of the house than ever before, and even dad seemed unusually irritated as of late.

"Mom, I don't want to get into your business, but I'd be careful with Jolene if I were you. She's like a ticking time bomb as of late...ready to explode at any minute. And, I hate to say it, but you do a pretty good job of getting under her skin just when she's about to explode," Abby said.

"Excuse me?" Mom replied.

"It's true. I'm not taking sides, I'm just stating a fact. The two of you aren't exactly getting along well these days. Last time I checked, you need her there to help with dad." Abby continued.

"I understand I need her help, but I've said it before and I'll say it again. I will not allow her to run amuck under my roof. Jolene is a wonderful nurse, and it's been nice to have her expertise around as we attempt to make life as comfortable as we can for your father with the dementia. However-"

"Oh, good Lord, why did you get her all fired up? I thought this was supposed to be a peaceful day at the beach," Rebecca said. Mom rolled her eyes at her.

"As I was saying, it has been wonderful having Jolene as an option instead of having to put your father in a nursing home, but I won't stand for all the drinking and disorderly living. I won't have it. Not under my roof. No ma'am." Mom repositioned herself in her Adirondack chair and grabbed a magazine. It was her way of dismissing the topic, which prompted Abby to do the same.

"Well, here's another topic for discussion. Payton, did you tell everyone about the visitor who stopped by the store this week?" Abby asked.

"Abby! Really?"

"What's the big deal? I didn't think you would care," Abby said.

"Well, I don't, really. I just thought I would decide to talk about it when I'm ready," I said.

"Talk about what? I thought you two were past the stage of keeping secrets. What's going on?" Rebecca asked.

"No one is keeping a secret. It literally just happened," I said.

There had to have been some rule of law among the Matthews women that stated thou shalt keep the drama going at all times. I planned on brushing the topic of Maxine under the rug and moving on with life. I felt sorry for the woman for committing to marrying such a low-life like Jack, but there was nothing I could do about it. If she didn't have the good sense to go with her gut instinct, that was on her, not me.

"Tell them, Payton. They may have some good advice to offer." Abby nudged.

"If you insist, although I'm not sure what good it will do."

I looked over at Alice, my mother-in-law, feeling somewhat embarrassed and wondering what she would think of me. One would think by now that stories involving my ex would truly be behind me.

"Jack's fiancé stopped by the store this week."

Rebecca began choking on her salsa dip and reached for her soda to clear her throat.

"What?" Mom said.

"You heard her right. I swear if I didn't know any better, I'd think Jack is intentionally trying to keep up with Payton," Abby said.

"That's probably pushing it too far, Abby. I doubt that I ever cross his mind. According to what she had to say, it sounds like he hasn't changed a bit. He's probably still out there being a ladies' man, and it's just getting underneath her skin, that's all."

"Why did she come by the store to see you? Or better yet, how does she even know who you are or where to find you?" Alice asked.

"Now, that's the million-dollar question." Rebecca chimed in, being an instigator as usual.

If looks could kill, someone would have to dial 911 on her behalf, I thought to myself.

"A few months ago, she wrote me a letter stating that she found my name in some old files that Jack had. She looked me up, knowing that I returned to Pelican Beach and found my name under the public listing for the store. Sadly, it doesn't end there. Apparently, she's getting cold feet about whether to proceed with marrying Jack. She mentioned something in the letter about him drinking, gambling, and I don't know... something about questioning his past," I said.

"Man, I bet you're glad he's a thing of the past. He sounds like bad news," Alice replied.

"Honestly, Alice. I stopped recognizing Jack toward the end of our marriage. I don't know who he was. He certainly wasn't the man I married," I explained.

"So, what does she want from you?" Mom asked.

"Well, she said they're in town for a conference and extended vacation. She just wants to talk. I get the impression she wants to ask me specifics about Jack, but I don't want to go there with her. There's a reason I call him my ex."

"I don't blame you, Payton. I thought it was pretty nervy of her to come to the store, if you ask me. You didn't respond to her letter and that should've been a clue that you didn't want to be bothered," Abby said.

"Was she pretty?" Rebecca asked.

"She wasn't ugly. She was soaked from head to toe from the storm. But even with raccoon eyes from her mascara, she was still drop dead gorgeous. Would you expect anything less from Jack? He looks like a freaking Ken doll, for goodness' sake. Guys like that usually have a good-looking woman on their arm," Abby said, speaking on my behalf.

As the oldest, Abby was good at looking out for us and offering sisterly advice. We were all close, and as a result we usually talked about everything. But this was one time where I preferred they'd dial down the conversation and let me handle things in my own way.

"Eh em, ladies, must we do this now? This is supposed to be a day of relaxation. Nobody is interested in hearing about Jack and Maxine," I said.

"I want to hear about it. This is way more interesting than anything they've been playing on General Hospital," Rebecca replied. Mom and Alice agreed and encouraged me to continue.

"I really don't know that there's much more to tell. She wants to talk, and I'm not interested in getting involved. It's that simple."

"Yeah, maybe... but here's something to consider. Perhaps if you talk to her, you can put this thing behind you once and for all. I mean, if she's in town for two weeks, do you really think you've seen the last of her? Probably not. Maybe it would be best to call her up and ask her to meet you at the store. Abby will be there with you, so you won't be alone. Is there really any harm in it?" Alice asked.

"Alice, I'm surprised to hear you suggest such a thing. To me, it seems like getting entangled in my ex-husband's business is asking for trouble, don't you think?"

"Well, it depends on how you look at it. When Cole was knee high to a duck, I had a situation slightly different from this one, but it taught me a lesson I'll never forget. Now, if you ever repeat this to Cole, I'll deny it ever happened," she said.

"Your secret is safe with me."

"Good. Like, I was saying, when Cole was just a young boy there was a woman who was in hot pursuit of his father. She didn't know that I was aware, and neither did he. I may have been a stay-at-home mother, but I wasn't an oblivious one. A woman knows when someone is trying to win her husband's affection. I waited until the time was right and addressed the issue head on. My husband, God rest his soul, wasn't aware that I planned on approaching her, and it was better off that way. I paid a visit to her home and had a nice long one-to-one conversation... you know, to make her aware that I wasn't sitting at home with my head buried in the sand and that I was well aware of her intensions with my husband. Payton, from that day on, it was the last time I ever had to speak to that woman again. Our conversation had a lasting impact, and that was a secret I kept to myself until now. Why do I share this story? It's because I believe sometimes you have to step in and nip things in the bud. You gotta deal with it head on before you find yourself amid an even greater problem. Is this woman a threat to your marriage? No, of course not. However, it seems like Jack and his business is a constant threat to you and your family and he never seems to go away. So, if it were me, I would deal with it once and for all," Alice said.

"How?" I asked.

"There're many ways you can go about it. Call her and talk with her... answer her questions if you'd like, or not... that part is up to you. But, whatever you do, make it clear to Maxine and even to Jack if necessary, that you no longer want to be contacted by either of them. Instead of telling us how much you don't want to have anything to do with him, tell them directly. That's the way to nip this thing in the bud once and for all," she said.

"Oh, I don't know, Alice. Talking to Jack means seeing him and that's just a little too close to comfort for me."

"Okay, well, then make your point clear to her. Either way, doing something is better than doing nothing at all. So far, look where that's gotten you. You ignored her letter, so she shows up unannounced at the store. What next? What if she goes through with marrying him and he has other business trips here in the future? Will it ever end?"

"You know, Payton, Alice is right. This could turn into an ongoing thing if you don't address it," Rebecca said.

Mom agreed with Rebecca, and Abby looked as if she was coming around to the idea. I, on the other hand, still had my reservations. Outside of her name I knew nothing about this woman, and the only thing I wanted to focus on was delivering healthy babies in a few weeks.

"So, you all actually think that talking to this woman is a good idea?" I asked.

"If I could intervene, Payton. I think nipping this in the bud is a fantastic idea. Think of it as doing what's best for your marriage." Mom suggested.

"I agree with your mother. Talk to Cole about it and see what he says. But, the main point I'm trying to get across is you need to nip this in the bud, that's all. It's time that you and Cole move on with your lives in peace. Period." Alice added.

"Pay, I'd have to agree. I know I was against it at first, but now that I'm looking at this from Alice's point of view, this needs to be put in check. You would never show up in his life the way he has in yours. Even if the shoe were on the other foot, you just wouldn't do it. You've moved on, and you have way too much class to behave this way. I'm with Alice, talk to this woman... but not for the sake of satisfying her needs... but the sake of laying down the law and kicking them out of your life for good." Abby insisted.

I stretched my feet out on the chaise lounge and pulled my hat down over my face. Somehow, dreams of a peaceful afternoon with the girls turned into all hearts and minds focused on my life. *I wish I never met Jack,* I thought to myself. *I wish I never knew he existed.*

JOLENE

*H*elen was at the beach and I was home, trying to indulge Will in conversation, while watching the Marlins play. He stretched out in his recliner with a throw across his feet and a scowled expression across his face. If there was any emotion to be expressed, it was bound to happen in front of the television set over sports.

"Will, it's nearly ninety degrees outside. Are you sure you don't want me to remove the throw from across your feet?"

"No." He grumbled.

"Well, you know Helen keeps the thermostat practically on seventy-eight degrees in the summer. I don't know how you can stand it, to be honest. There simply aren't enough fans in this place to keep me from having a hot flash and here you are with a blanket across your legs."

He continued staring at the television screen, ignoring me completely.

"Sometimes I think about walking around here in the buff.

Maybe then Helen would consider lowering the temperature. I bet that would get her attention." I laughed to myself.

"I just don't know how you deal with her, to be honest. If I was married to somebody like that after all these years, I'd lose my mind." I continued.

Will didn't say anything. Not that I expected him to.

"I guess now is a good time to talk and let you know what's been on my mind. You're pretty quiet, so I know my secret is safe with you. Plus, I really think you ought to know first, since we spend all of our time together. I've been thinking about moving back to Jacksonville. You see the way Helen and I bump heads and well... I think it's time. It seems only fitting that I would return to my hometown and get back to my roots," I said.

As usual, Will remained fixated on the game, occasionally flinching ever so slightly when his team didn't score.

"The thing is... I may have been hasty to pack up my things, thinking that I could start a new life out here. My responsibilities became too overwhelming after George passed, and I panicked. In hindsight, there were probably other options for me. If I'd just taken the time to explore those options, I may have been able to stay. I have nobody to blame for that but myself. It's not like Helen twisted my arm to come here or anything. Plus, I'll admit, you can be stubborn at times, but so can I. For the most part we've always gotten along well. Even back during the days when we all used to take road trips together. Remember that? Those were the good ole days, weren't they Will?" I asked.

He mumbled something in between nodding off to sleep.

"Let the truth be told, Helen and I simply don't get along, anymore. Going on vacation together and living together are two different things. If I have to continue on like this, I'm liable to lose control... and I know you'd never want me to do such a thing. Hell, I wouldn't even want to go that far while I'm in my right mind, but let me get a few glasses of brandy in me and anything is possible."

Just then, the sound of keys dropping into a dish interrupted my thought pattern.

"Hello, Jolene," Helen said.

"Helen, I didn't hear you come in."

"How could you? I'm sure the volume on the television has something to do with that," she said, while reaching for the remote.

"Did everyone enjoy their time at the beach this afternoon?"

"We did."

Helen adjusted the cover on Will's feet and bent over, kissing him on the forehead. His eyebrows raised for a moment, only to return to his comfortable resting position. She seemed quiet, maybe even a little stoic, which made me question if she heard me talking to Will.

"How are the ladies doing?" I asked.

"They're fine. Alice asked about you."

"Oh, that's nice. Next time you see her you'll have to send my regards."

"Mm hmm," Helen responded.

"Something wrong?"

"I was going to ask you the same, Jolene. I overheard you telling Will that you plan to return to Jacksonville. Were you planning on saying anything to me about it?" she asked.

"Of course I was going to tell you... when I was ready. I just recently decided that it's the best thing for me to do. I'm still sorting through the details, but I wouldn't just up and leave without saying anything."

"Well, that's nice to know. This is a big deal, Jolene. We depend on you to be here for Will. Without your help, there's no way I can care for him by myself. If we can't find another reliable nurse, then my options are pretty limited," she said.

"I understand that. I promise I will not leave without giving you adequate time to find a replacement, Helen. I've never been so insensitive, and I won't start now."

I could tell she was displeased yet silenced, not really knowing what to say.

"Helen, I came here intending to stay and making a new life for myself. But, to be honest, I haven't been able to accomplish that. I'm unhappy. You and I bicker all the time and if we're not bickering, then all I ever do is work," I said.

"Oh, I get it. So you don't enjoy taking care of Will, anymore?"

"That's not it at all. Have you been listening to anything that I just said? I don't have a life, and I also don't want to bicker with you anymore, Helen. Everything in your life is in order. You have it made. You live a plush life here at the cottage with ocean views. You can come and go as you please and do all the things you've been accustomed to doing before I arrived. Why? Because you know I'll be here to care for Will twenty-four hours a day, seven days a week. But, what about me? My personal life consists of hanging out at the inn a couple of times a week and spending the rest of my time here."

"I didn't realize that you blame me for your personal life or lack thereof," she responded.

"I don't blame you. I've just come to learn that I need my space. I need to get back to focusing on what makes me happy.

There should be boundaries and a healthy balance between your work and personal life... and let's face it... those boundaries are not in place for me. Plus, I'm tired of being scolded for how I choose to live my life. I know I can be a handful, I get it. But, I'm a grown woman, Helen. Most of all, we've always had a loving relationship. Me, you, Will... and even George when he was living. We were all tight like glue. I don't want to ruin that." I pleaded.

Helen sat beside me on the couch, kicked up her feet and faced the view of the sunset through her living room window.

"I get it, Jolene." She gave me a pat on the leg while continuing to look at the sunset.

"I'm not as out of touch as you think I am. I've noticed for quite some time now that you're not happy. It's like you've been searching for something but you haven't been able to find it. In the beginning I passed it off as you missing George or figuring you needed more time to settle in. Don't get me wrong, you'll always miss George because that's human nature. But, that's not at the root of what's been bothering you. You need a place to call your own. I'll be the first to admit that I'm particular about the way I do things around the house, and well... I'm sure that's been driving you nuts, hasn't it?"

"Nuts is an understatement." I laughed.

We hadn't talked like this in a long while. It felt good to get everything out in the open.

"Thanks, Jolene. I can always count on you to give it to me straight." She teased.

"No problem, that's what I'm here for."

Helen contemplated for a moment.

"Was I really plucking your nerves that bad?" she asked.

"We've been plucking each other's nerves, but that doesn't

change the fact that we're family, and we love each other. Whether I'm here or back home, that will never change," I said.

"Aww, Jolene, I think that's the nicest thing you've ever said to me."

"It's true." I smiled.

Will woke up in time to catch the final inning of the game while Helen and I spoke about future plans.

"Do you have any idea when you'll head back or where you'll live? It's been a while since you had to navigate Jacksonville on your own. You have a lot to consider," Helen said.

"I figured you'd need a couple of months to make new arrangements. Maybe I'll take a weekend trip here and there to get reacquainted. I was thinking it might be nice to find a rental suitable for me and maybe a small pet to keep me company."

"How's your guy friend, David, going to feel about you leaving?" she asked.

"I'm sure he'll be thrilled. He'll have one less person chewing his ear off at the inn when he's trying to close up for the night."

"That's interesting. I always thought the two of you were starting to get a little close." Helen nudged me, implying more than she was willing to say.

"Close? Me and David? Nahh. We're just friends who get together to share stories over drinks. I had to find some way to enjoy my nightcap without getting the third degree." I teased.

"I wouldn't be so certain if I were you. As much as you talk about him, he sounds like more than a friend to me," she said.

I had to admit, I spent most of my free time with him whenever he was in town, but as an outlet. A means to get out of the house. David was younger and handsome and could command the attention of just about anybody he wanted to, really. Occasionally, he shared stories about his family, his childhood, and what life was like as a loner, but never in my wildest dreams did I associate him as someone of interest, or someone who would be interested in me.

"No, no, Helen. You've got it all wrong. It was probably me just flapping off at the mouth about one thing or another. Just passing the time, really. There's nothing more to it than that."

"If you say so. Well, we can't continue to sit here and expect dinner to cook itself. I'm going to heat up the leftovers. Can I get you anything?" Helen asked.

"I'll come help you. But first, Helen... I just want to thank you for being so understanding. I didn't think you'd take the news as well as you did. Plus, to have you walk in and overhear me complaining... that wasn't fair."

Helen's eyes teared up as she walked with me arm in arm toward the kitchen.

"We're family, Jolene. That doesn't mean things will always be perfect between us, but no matter what, we're here to support one another."

She faced me, placing her hand over mine.

"If returning to Jacksonville is what you need in order to be happy, then we're going to make that happen. We'll get a plan in place for Will, and everything will work out just fine. I know it will," she said.

"Thank you, Helen."

That evening I listened to the sound of the record player softly soothing as I contemplated my future and prepared to meet David. It was funny how life worked. I didn't expect Helen to be so understanding, and now that she was, I was free to make plans, yet I wasn't sure what to do.

Heading toward the Veranda instead of the bar felt awkward to say the least. David usually had my favorite beverage ready for me on the rocks, and he was kind enough to not expect anything in return, except to spend a little time talking about the day's events. I wasn't sure what he had in mind, but I followed his instructions to meet him at seven o'clock sharp.

"There she is, right on time, as usual," he said as he pulled out a chair to a table lit by candlelight.

"This is mighty fancy for just a cocktail and conversation, David. Who's covering the bar tonight?" I asked.

"Don't you worry about who's covering the bar. I have everything under control. Did you forget I own the place and have to stay on top of who's doing what around here?"

"I know. Even so, I don't understand why we're over here. Can't we just enjoy our usual nightcap without all the fancy linen and candles?"

"See, that's the problem, Jolene. You're always investing so much of your time in others, you do not know how to invest in yourself. It's a treat. Just sit with me... relax and enjoy yourself."

I guess he had a point. Plus, as I glanced over at the bar, it was particularly crowded with a bunch of women making a commotion over a bride-to-be. It was probably one of those bachelorette parties. That kind of noise I could do without.

"Please have a seat with me," he said.

"Alright. But, I won't be staying long. I have so many things running around in my head tonight, I can hardly think straight."

"What wrong?" he asked.

"Ah, nothing a good night's rest can't cure. I'll tell you about it after I order my first drink. Let's start with you. How was your day? Did you sketch out a few plans for selling your other businesses like we agreed?"

"As a matter of fact, I did," he replied.

"Really? Do tell."

The server placed the menus on the table and shared the specials for the evening.

"I'll just have a glass of brandy on the rocks, please," I said.

"Surely you're going to eat with me?"

"You just told me to meet you at the Veranda. You didn't tell me we were having dinner. I already ate with Helen and Will at the house," I explained.

"I didn't think I had to spell it out. We're known for serving meals at the Veranda. You ought to know that. Your family used to own the place. Will you at least have dessert?"

"Eh, why not? I'll try your chocolate mousse," I said to the server.

David ordered a full meal and cracked a few jokes with the server as he passed the menu back. I could hear Helen's voice in the back of my mind just as clear as day, reminding me, *How do you think your friend David will feel about you moving back to Jacksonville?*

When they were done talking, he reverted his attention back to me.

"So, tell me all about it. What kind of plan did you come up with?" I asked.

"You're not going to believe this, Jolene. I made a couple of calls, just to put some feelers out there, and it turns out some of the local owners may be interested in buying. I have one guy who begged me not to make another call until we can schedule an appointment to go over the numbers. Can you believe that?"

"That's fantastic. I'm not surprised. From what I can tell you really know a lot about the hospitality industry. I'm sure it's become clear to other businesses in the community."

"Thank you."

"What about your third location? Do you think you'll be able to find someone for that, too?" I asked.

"Not yet. It's probably wise that I focus on selling one place at a time. I may take the traditional route and hire a realtor for that one. Either way, the thought of settling down here in Florida makes me happy."

"I'll bet. You deserve it," I responded.

"I appreciate it, but that's not why I invited you here tonight. I actually asked you here just to spend some uninterrupted time with you. I thought it might be nice to sit down and talk over a meal. Of course, I think next time I need to do a better job and let you know if a meal is going to be involved."

I chuckled. Then it dawned on me, why would he be planning a meal, or a next time to begin with? David knew I was a laid back kind of woman from the countryside of Jacksonville. Fine dining and candlelight dinners didn't fit the bill for someone like me.

"That's kind of you, David, but you know I'm just as happy as I can be sitting right over there in my favorite seat at the bar. If it weren't for the noisy party of women, I'd probably be sitting over there right now. I sure am going to miss this place." The words slipped out before I had time to consider what I was saying.

"What do you mean you're going to miss this place? You're in here at least two to three times a week." He laughed.

The look of innocence on David's face as he sought to understand was telling. As many times as I sat and talked with him about how miserable I was, he didn't get it. In a little while I would be leaving Pelican Beach for good.

"I planned on telling you about it tonight. When I mentioned I had a lot on my mind, I was referring to the talk I had with Helen about moving back to Jacksonville," I said.

The server placed our beverages down and promised to return in a short while with our order. David let out a small sigh and wore an expression of disappointment.

"Wow, when we spoke about dreaming again, and putting plans in motion, I did not know it would involve you leaving. Are you sure this is what you want to do?" he asked.

"I'm sure that I haven't been happy. I'm also sure that I don't fit in around here."

"Jolene, what would make you say a thing like that? Is it that you don't fit in or you've never tried to lay a path of your own?" he asked.

"What do you mean? All I ever do is work, take a few hours off at night, get up, and start the same routine all over again."

"My point exactly. There are other ways to go about establishing a life for yourself here. What about finding a little place to rent and setting real work hours with Helen? Did you ever consider that?" he asked.

"No, but-"

"Before you insert a but hold on... think about it. When we first met, you never complained about Pelican Beach. You were always taken back by the small beach community, the inn, and everything the area offered. What happened to that Jolene? She's gotta be in there somewhere. You haven't really given this place the chance that it deserves. The chance that you deserve for yourself, Jolene."

David reached his hand across the table and placed it over

mine. It was the first time he made a physical gesture that showed how much he cared. I found myself staring at the pores in his fair skin, and got lost in the warmth of his gentle touch.

"Jolene," he said.

I slowly withdrew my hand, straightening up in the chair, ready to defend my decision.

"That may have been who I was when we first met. But, after thinking things over and calculating the cost, I think it would be best for myself and everyone else if I head back home. Helen is being more supportive than I ever imagined she would. I think it's my best option at this point."

"Who's going to look out for you when you get back to Jacksonville?" he asked.

"I can reconnect with some of my old neighbors and folks I know from the community. "

"What about family? Folks who will look after you if you're sick or if you're ever in need?" he asked.

"I'll figure something out. Hey, if I didn't know any better, it sounds like you're actually going to miss me." I teased.

"I am. I guess your news was just a bit unexpected, that's all. If you feel like this is what's best for you, there's nothing I can say to stop you. I just think it's pretty sad you never gave Pelican Beach a chance."

"David, that's not fair. And why are you being such a Debbie Downer? We ought to be making a toast. There's so much to celebrate. We both have a bright future on the horizon. Come on... lift your glass. Let's toast to new beginnings."

I held my glass up, waiting for David to join me. All he could manage to do was tap the glass and take his first sip with little to no enthusiasm.

PAYTON

*a*fter dinner my step-daughter Emmie disappeared upstairs to get into her nightly ritual of talking to her best friends. It was their summer evening ritual if they weren't spending the night at one another's house. Cole lit a few torches out back and massaged my lower back and feet to relieve me of my discomfort.

"Cole, I couldn't make it through this pregnancy without your massages. Sometimes muscles in my lower back ache so much I could scream," I said.

"If somebody would listen to her husband and cut back on her hours at the store, it might not be as bad."

"I pull up a stool every chance I get. It still doesn't make a difference. It's time for these girls to come out. I love them dearly but they're doing a number on my body." I groaned.

"We're almost there, babe. Before you know it you'll be holding them in your arms. Maybe then you'll listen to me and slow down a bit. Actually, you'll have no choice." He laughed.

"True. Come here. Sit beside me and tell me all about your day."

He snuggled up close. We were still like teenagers in love, though I felt like I was carrying an entire girl scout troop inside me.

"Hmm, let's see. We tied up a few loose ends with the kitchen renovation this morning, so that job is complete. I also reviewed a proposal for a commercial job, although I'm not sure that I'm going to entertain it," he said.

"Why not?"

"Because it would require all hands on deck to tackle this project and a lot of hours spent away from the house during the day. I want to be here for you and the twins. You're my number one priority, Payton, you know that." He caressed my hair as we continued to talk.

"Yeah, but we anticipated that you would take a couple of weeks off and then gradually phase back to your regular work schedule. You can't figure out a way for the guys to cover for you toward the beginning of the job and maybe you manage things from behind the scenes for a few weeks?" I asked.

"I wish. Don't get me wrong, the money would be great, but the time spent with you and our baby girls is priceless. I won't be able to get that time back."

"You know what?" I asked.

"Hmm."

"You're already the best girl-dad, so I know you are going to be the most amazing with the twins."

He soaked up the compliment with a huge smile.

"Cole, there's something I want you to know," I said.

"What's that?"

"It hasn't gone unnoticed that you've been super patient

with me, as my body is going through so many pregnancy changes. I know you've been missing our alone time. Instead of complaining, you've been right there by my side, taking good care of me. When this is behind us I'm going to make it up to you." I smiled.

"I'm happy to take care of you, babe. It's my job as your husband," he said.

"Oh, so you don't want me to make it up to you?"

"I didn't say that. The mere thought of being close to you again is making my head spin. But, until then, don't you worry about me. A cold shower will straighten me right up." He chuckled.

"What about you? I want to hear all about your day at the store, plus, you never caught me up on your visit with the ladies yesterday," he said.

"Everything at the store is fine. I finally secured part-time help for Abby, which makes me feel good. I was pushing my luck. I should've had someone weeks ago, but you know how I am about hiring people to work at the store. They have to be the right fit."

"Who did you decide to go with?" he asked.

"I chose the woman with ten years of photography experience. She's been working as a freelancer, just like I did, and she's basically looking for some part-time income to hold her over when business is slow. She says she likes the flexibility to continue freelance work. Cole, she's really good. Her portfolio was filled with amazing photos from a Santa Barbara wedding, a Morraco photoshoot, and a gorgeous wedding she was hired to do right here in Pelican Beach."

"That's wonderful. I'm sure Abby can help train her and perhaps you can reduce your hours a little?" he asked.

"Not so fast. We agreed, as long as I felt up to it, that I would continue to work, remember?"

"Yes, boss." He smirked.

"So, what kind of gossip was being spread by the Matthews women at Sunday afternoon lunch? Normally, by now you would've covered everything from soup to nuts." Cole teased.

"You're so silly. Believe it or not, there was no gossiping going on this time. We just enjoyed each other's company, ate, laughed, and laid out in the sun. Well, they did at least. I hid under an umbrella, but I still had a good time."

"No gossip? As in...none. Uh, no. Sorry, I'm not buying it. Either someone asked you to swear to secrecy, or you're keeping secrets from me. There's not a time where you don't come home with a full rundown of the hot topics shared by you and your sisters," he said.

"I guess I developed that bad habit, didn't I? Now, you've come to expect updates. That's terrible, Cole. You're just as bad as the rest of us."

"Mm hmm." He moaned.

"Well, for the sake of being transparent, we were talking about a visitor that showed up at Picture Perfect last week."

"That's interesting." He said.

"I know, it completely slipped my mind until Abby brought it up at the beach on Sunday. It's really not that big of a deal."

An expression of doubt flashed across Cole's face. In the short time that we've been married, the man knew me very well, sometimes better than I knew myself. If there was one thing I wasn't good at it was lying to him, even if it was in the name of protecting his feelings.

"If it's not a big deal, then tell me. Who was it?" he asked.

"Maxine Waters, Jack's fiancé. They're in town on business

and an extended vacation. She stopped by the store to tell me she's in town for two weeks and she'd like to meet to ask me a few questions."

"Regarding?" Cole sounded annoyed.

"Regarding the letter she sent months back... I don't know... perhaps regarding some reservations she's having about marrying Jack? Either way, she seems pretty certain that talking to me can help resolve some of her unrest. I told her I didn't want to get involved, but the girl seems pretty desperate for help."

"I have to say, I feel kind of bummed that your sisters and our mothers knew about this before me, Payton," he said.

"I know, but in all fairness, I planned on forgetting about it completely. Abby's the one who brought it up. She was there the day Maxine stopped by."

"Your safety means everything to me. I want to know when things like this happen. Promise me you'll tell me next time?"

"I promise. But, honestly, Cole, I didn't sense one ounce of a threat coming from this woman. She seemed like someone who's just desperate to know the truth... maybe even fearful, but certainly not a threat," I said.

"How can you be so sure?"

"Because I recognize that feeling. I know first-hand what it's like to doubt the one you love," I said.

Cole gave me a look out of the corner of his eye.

"No, not you, silly. I know I can trust you. I'm referring to Jack. I remember that feeling. Seeing the desperation in her eyes gave me flashbacks to those not-so-pleasant days."

"All the more reason you shouldn't have anything to do with her," he said as he rubbed his hand across my belly.

I wanted to melt into a puddle at the idea of sharing what I was really thinking with Cole. After talking with his mother, Alice, I decided that I would speak to Maxine. I knew he would struggle to understand my reasoning. I needed to be careful and choose my words wisely.

"I don't know how to say this, Cole, but after talking to your mother and giving it some thought, I actually think I want to speak to Maxine." I hesitated.

"My mother? What does she have to do with this?"

"Well, Alice along with the others gave me wise advice, about dealing with this head on. She said it might be a good idea to just talk with her, especially since she's been rather persistent to write and then show up at the store. At first I didn't see the point, but the more I sit with the idea, I think it makes sense. I can meet with her and then clarify that reaching out to me is off limits. Of course, I would not make this decision without involving you," I said.

Cole relaxed in his chair and allowed his hand to fall by his waist side. If I had to guess, he didn't look like he was so keen on the idea.

"Talk to me, babe. I don't want this to ruin our evening. I just wanted to be honest with you, that's all," I said.

He sighed aloud and extended his hand out to me.

"My initial thought... I don't like it. I don't want you to have anything to do with Maxine, just because she's connected to your ex. You can call it me just being a man, I guess. But, the one thing I know without a shadow of a doubt is that I trust you. I can't say that I understand it, but if you want to talk with her, who am I to stand in the way? Plus, my mother, your mother, and your sisters are pretty wise women. Well, I take that back, Rebecca has always been rather special," he said.

I whacked him on the arm for talking about my sister, but if the truth be told, he was right.

"Payton, seriously, they're all pretty wise, so I trust they wouldn't give you the wrong advice. I'm supportive of whatever you decide to do. Just fill me in and perhaps Abby can be there with you just in case things don't turn out as expected," he said.

"Cole."

"Yes," he said with a soft smile.

"Thank you for always being so supportive. Even when you'd rather not be."

"That doesn't exist. I always want to be supportive of you, Payton," he said, while intertwining his fingers with mine.

"You know, Cole. After we say goodnight to Emmie, I may need a little assistance with drawing a nice, warm bath. Would you mind helping me?" I asked with a flirtatious smile.

"Would I mind? Are you kidding me? Darlin, just say the word and I'll be there with bells on."

I knocked on Emmie's door hoping to catch up on her day before she turned in for the night. With the first year of middle school behind her, she was growing up so fast. Just yesterday she was inviting me for milkshakes and drawing pictures together. Now her social life was a big priority, but thankfully she always remained sweet.

"Come in." She called.

"Hey, Emms," I said, peeking my head inside.

"I thought I'd stop by and hang out with you for a while if you weren't too busy. I miss our girl time together."

"Sure, make yourself comfortable on the bean bag," she said.

"I wish I could. I'm afraid if I get down there, I might not get back up. How about I hang out at the bottom of your bed?"

"Cool."

"So, talk to me, girlie. Outside of tennis lessons you have a ton of free time this summer. I was wondering if you'd like to sign up for horseback riding or maybe help Aunt Abby at the shop once or twice a week?"

"Hmm, well, I don't want to hurt Aunt Abby's feelings, but I'd really love to try horseback riding. After I'm done with my lessons, I can come home and help with the twins," she said.

"Abby doesn't know, so don't worry about it. And, you're right, I'm going to need all the extra help I can get. How's your diaper changing skills?" I asked.

"I don't know, but I'm sure I can figure it out. Unless it's number two. In that case, I'll call you or dad for some help." Emmie laughed.

"Oh, no, you don't. I read somewhere in the big sister handbook that states you must change diapers regardless of what's inside."

"There's no such thing as a big sister handbook." She emphasized.

"Alright. We'll see to it that you have something to do to help out with your sisters. What's your friends up to this summer?"

"You mean, what's my only friend, Melissa, up to this summer? Her family is going on vacation to Hawaii next month," Emmie responded.

"Emms, why is Melissa your only friend? What's the matter?"

"The other girls stopped talking to me. They think I was involved in spreading a mean rumor, but I wasn't. I had nothing to do with it, but they don't believe me. I swear all the girls at Pelican Beach Middle School are the meanest girls I've ever met. All of them except Melissa. She's the only one who believes I would never do such a thing," she said.

"Oh, for heaven's sake this is ridiculous. Why didn't you say something before now? I can put an end to this by talking to their mothers."

"That's exactly why I didn't bring it up. If they can't be nice to me on their own, without their parents getting involved, then they're really not my friends anyway, Mom. I'm happy with just hanging out with Melissa, really," she said.

Emmie spoke like a girl who was well beyond her years. She knew what she wanted out of life and being associated with the mean girls wasn't it.

"Are you sure? You've always had this way of not wanting your father and me to get involved, but we're here for you, Emms. That's what parents do."

"I know, but I can handle this. Let's face it. Would you really want me to be friends with a bunch of stuck up girls, anyway?" she asked.

"You're right. I sure do admire your sense of maturity, Emmie. I don't think I was nearly as mature as you are when I was your age."

"I think it comes from growing up around a bunch of adults. Dad used to always say that when mom was alive they planned on having a lot of kids. Of course, that never happened, but I'm happy he gets to make his dream come true with you, and I'm happy I'm older. That way the twins can look up to me," she said.

"Aww, Emms, I know the girls will. Even as your step-mom, I look up to you, and I couldn't agree more with what you said earlier about those girls who were supposed to be friends. If they can't see the value in your friendship, you don't need them. You and Melissa might want to introduce yourselves to the sweet new girl who just moved in down the street. She looks to be about your age and she has much younger siblings. You know what that means, don't you?" I asked.

"Yep, she probably can offer me tons of advice on being the oldest in the house and she probably needs to hang out around people her own age every once in a while."

"Exactly. I say tomorrow we get in the kitchen and put your baking skills to work. We can make a welcome basket filled with your delicious cookies. How does that sound to you?" I asked.

"Sounds good to me."

"Good. It's a plan. In the meantime, I'm going to get ready for bed. It's been a long day and these feet of mine need rest. Make sure you don't stay up too late. You have tennis practice first thing in the morning, and you know coach likes to be prompt. I love you, Emms."

"I love you, too."

JOLENE

By Monday afternoon I was back at the inn, earlier than my usual time to see if I could talk to David. I'd never known him to be as sour as he was last night after I shared the news. Frank, his assistant, was sweeping the floors, keeping the place tidy as he always did, and just a few customers were passing by in bathing suits, heading toward the pool.

"Hey, Frank, how's it going?" I asked.

"Hi, Jolene, oh, it's going well now. Can't say it was that way this morning when the water heater stopped working."

"Oh, no. I'll bet David had a fit." I nodded.

"More like a conniption, but he's got a guy down there taking a look at it now. He says it should be up and running in no time. Thankfully, it happened early enough this morning where most of the folks staying at the inn were still asleep. Now, I'd imagine everyone will start heading straight to the beach or the pool, so the worst is behind us. It shouldn't be too bad. How's your day coming along so far?" he asked.

"I can't complain. Just running a few errands for Helen and Will. I thought I'd stop by and see if I could catch David, but if he's busy-"

"Stay here for a moment. I know he mentioned they were almost done. I'll see if I can get him for you," he said.

"No... I don't want to bother him. It's not that important. It can wait until the next time I stop by."

"Are you sure? He's just in the boiler room. It will only take a minute for me to run down and yell for him," Frank replied.

"It's okay. Thank you, anyway. If I don't see you have a good afternoon, Frank."

"Okay, you, too."

While digging into my purse for the keys, I turned around and caught a glimpse of the tip of David's cowboy boots coming toward me. It didn't matter what the temperature was, you could always count on him wearing denim jeans, a belt with a big buckle, boots, and his Texas cowboy hat. I always thought of him as a Floridian with Texas charm.

"David, there you are. Frank told me you were downstairs in the boiler room," I said.

"I was, but everything is fixed now. I was just checking the grounds to see to it that everything is in order. What brings you here this early? Is everything all right?" he asked.

"Yes, everything is fine. I just stopped by to-"

I hesitated for a moment. *Why did I stop by?* It was probably because I was carrying this guilt associated with his reaction to me leaving. I wanted to sort things out and make sure everything was still good between us.

"You stopped by to...?" he said.

"Oh, I was just in the area... on my way to run errands, actually. I thought I would stop by to say hi, but when I found out you were busy, I decided not to bother you."

"Mm hmm," he replied.

"It's true. I wanted to check and see how you were doing after our little chat. You didn't seem like yourself after I shared the news."

He looked beyond me, into the distance, appearing weighed down with something on his mind.

"Is it that obvious?" he asked.

"Well, yes. I really wish you'd tell me what's bothering you. It's like you're mad at me for moving or something. I don't know, but whatever it is, it's driving me crazy. I've got enough on my mind without worrying about one more thing."

He waited in silence for a moment and then motioned for me to walk with him along a path that led through the grounds of the inn. Outside of the occasional group that passed by with beach towels in hand, it was just the two of us.

"This is probably selfish of me to say but I don't want you to leave, Jolene." He turned and faced me, causing me to smile nervously.

"Is that what you've been worried about all this time? I'll be back to visit. I won't stay away indefinitely. My family is here, you're here. My nightcaps won't be the same. I'll have to come and have an occasional drink with you for old time's sake." I laughed.

"Jolene, I'm being serious."

"So am I. What's gotten into you, David?"

Before I could say another word, he engulfed my lips in his. Mentally, I questioned what was happening, but physically it was so good I couldn't stop. I felt the palm of his hand gently graze across my back, pulling me closer. Instead of resisting, I succumbed to the stroke of his touch, which was soon interrupted by the sound of children playing nearby.

"Eh em, uh... Okay," I said, while repositioning myself.

"I didn't see that coming." I continued.

He tipped his hat off to the family passing by and then motioned for us to continue walking.

"I didn't see it coming, either."

I stopped in my tracks and looked at him.

"I'm being sincere. I have feelings for you, Jolene. Feelings that run deeper than some casual attraction, but I didn't plan on kissing you."

He paused again, this time taking me by the hand.

"Jolene, if you left here without me revealing my genuine feelings for you, I don't think I could live with myself. Since the day we met, you've been like nourishment to my soul... you kept me company when I was lonely, you've been like a best friend to me, and you even welcomed me into the family for the holidays when I had nowhere to go. Even now, you're encouraging me to go after my dreams, and helping me pave the path for the future life that I want to live here in Pelican Beach. No one has ever done that for me before... no one but you. When we're around each other, it feels good. It feels like I'm home," he said.

"But-"

"No buts. Listen to me, Jolene. It may not have been our intention to be anything more than two people keeping each other company at the inn. But, for me, it's developed into something more. Something that I want to explore with you. And, before you say anything about me being younger, I don't care about that and neither should you. Once you get to be in your fifties and sixties, the age difference doesn't mean a hill of beans, and you know it."

He stroked my hair out of the way. I had to admit; the man was giving me goose bumps. A feeling I hadn't experienced since George was alive.

"I think about you all the time, Jolene. I think you and I have a special connection... we're a perfect fit that can't be denied. I was going to share my feelings with you when I told you about potentially settling here in Pelican Beach, but your news caught me so off guard... I just couldn't find the words."

I gathered my composure.

"Ahh, now it all makes sense," I responded.

Again David looked off into the distance, looking rather flush in the face.

"Tell me you aren't the least bit curious to know where this could lead? And, if you aren't curious, you can tell me that, too. Maybe it's just me on an island by myself feeling this way," he said.

"David."

A million thoughts ran through my mind, but none of them made enough sense to articulate. I clenched my keys, leaving marks in the palm of my hand.

"I don't know what to say. I wasn't expecting this. I didn't see it coming," I said.

He adjusted his hat while turning in the direction to head back to the inn.

"Right. I guess it wasn't fair of me to spring this on you out of nowhere. A pretty selfish move on my part, I suppose. It's like you said, you have enough to worry about."

"David."

"No... it's true. I apologize for coming on too strong and

making things awkward for you. I say we just put this behind us so you can get back to planning your return to Jacksonville."

"David... don't do this. This is not the way our time together is supposed to end. I haven't even set a date yet. I promised Helen I'd give her some time to make arrangements for Will. There's still plenty of time left for me to come and hang out with you here at the bar," I responded.

"I won't stop you. You're always welcome to come here. In the meantime, it's probably best I head back before someone comes looking for me."

He tipped his hat toward me and returned to the inn. I felt like a complete idiot. It was the first time I was at a loss for words.

Later that evening I made a few phone calls to put feelers out to a few of the old neighbors. I hadn't been able to erase the conversation I had with David out of my mind or the kiss... but if I was going to make any progress with getting back home, I needed to lay that aside for now and keep pressing forward.

"Naomi, is that you? It's Jolene, it's been so long I almost didn't recognize your voice. How are you?"

"Jolene Ferguson, I'm wonderful. I can't believe I'm hearing your voice on the other end of this telephone line. I don't know whether to be excited or worried. Is everything okay?" she asked.

"Oh, yes. Everything is fine. I should be ashamed of myself, taking so long to reach out to you."

"I understand. I'm just as much to blame. I have your cell phone number. I could've easily called by now. I just assumed you were busy with the family. I know my days have been filled with watching the grandkids. I honestly can't tell one day from the next. How's William and Helen doing?"

"They're coming along. Will is still battling with dementia but we're all pitching in to make things as easy as we can for him," I said.

"I'm sorry to hear that but I know they're glad to have you."

My mind drifted to flashbacks of helping Will over the last year and a half. It seemed like just yesterday I arrived with my bags in hand ready to help him return to his optimal state of well being.

"Jolene, are you still there?" she asked.

"Yes, yes. I'm still here. Naomi, I called you because ... well, I don't know how to put this other than to be blunt, but I called because I'm making arrangements to come back to Jacksonville. I was wondering how things have been in the neighborhood since I left. Specifically, I was wondering about my old house. Has anyone taken over the place and moved in?" I asked.

I never divulged all of the details with the family, but my finances were in need of a lot of repair when I packed my things and left. I ended up walking away from the house, handing it over to whoever would come and claim it. Naomi lived across the street from me and knew George well. I knew she would understand.

"The house sat vacant for almost a year before the bank stepped in and sold it to some investors. The neighborhood endured four long months of banging and knocking and hauling things back and forth. It's my understanding they gutted the place from top to bottom...new wood floors, master bath, new roof, new fencing. You'd barely recognize the place, Jolene."

I drew in a deep breath and grabbed a handkerchief.

"Is it up for sale now? I was thinking I could work out a deal to rent or lease to own the place if it was still available. Sure, it may take some getting used to the new decor and all, but it's the memories that mean the most to me. The four walls of that home hold a lot of memories that a couple of house flippers can't easily erase no matter what they've done to the place," I said.

"Sadly, Jolene, they sold it to a young couple just a little over a month ago. He's an engineer at the local plant and she's a kindergarten teacher. They're expecting their first child and wanted a backyard for their child to run and play in when she grows up. I'm sorry to be the bearer of such bad news."

I don't know why it felt like I was reliving the moment all over again when the nurse told me that George didn't make it. My heart hurt that day, just as it did now. It wouldn't make sense to anyone, not even Naomi. I was the one who gave up the house...but I didn't want to. I had no other choice. Even though it was silly of me to think I'd be able to live there again, I still had hope, until now.

"It's not your fault, Naomi. I was just curious, that's all. If you wouldn't mind keeping me abreast of any rentals that may become available in the area, I sure would appreciate it," I said.

"I'd be happy to."

"By the way, how's Sue Ellen and the girls doing?" I asked.

"They're all doing just fine. You know my daughter, she's constantly on the go and has those girls on a busy schedule as well. I don't know how they do it."

"I can imagine. You tell them all I said hello. And again, thank you for keeping an eye out for me, Naomi. I would imagine in the next month I'll be making plans to come down and visit. Maybe we can meet for lunch and catch up?"

"I'd love that. Glad you're moving back, Jolene. The old neighborhood hasn't been the same since you left," she said.

"Thank you, love. Talk to you soon."

"Bye, bye."

I laid the phone down on the receiver with a heavy heart. *What did you expect, Jolene?* I thought to myself. *That's part of the problem. You're too busy holding on to the past to even begin to make room for the future.*

I could feel the breeze from my bedroom window picking up. I turned off the lights and sat in the rocking chair, listening to the wind whistling over the rocks and sand. Tonight I didn't want to think about anything, I didn't want to feel anything. I just wanted to lose myself in the peace and tranquility of the evening.

ABBY

"*P*ayton, I've watched you pick up the phone and hang it up at least a thousand times. What's going on with you?" I asked.

"I don't know what to do," she said, while hanging up the phone again.

"About what?"

"Calling Maxine. I'd made up my mind I was going to do it. I even talked to Cole who was surprisingly supportive, more than likely because he knows how hard-headed I can be, but something tells me I'm in over my head this time, Abby. I probably just need to leave it alone and get back to focusing on training our new employee later on this week to prepare for maternity leave," she responded.

"Um, no. I will be focused on training our new employee. You will just be here for moral support and to remind me of anything I may be forgetting. As for Maxine, you need to deal with that situation before it blossoms out of control. If you don't talk to her now, it will only spiral into more letters, phone calls, pop in visits, and so forth. No way. I won't stand for it. I say schedule something casual at the inn. Tell her you'll meet her for lunch or something."

"I'm not having lunch with her. That's too much. Plus, Cole and I agreed you need to be there so, sorry. We either meet here at the shop or not at all," Payton said.

"Fine. Set up something here. Either way, get it over with." I marched over to the counter, dialed the number on the piece of paper she had in hand, and passed the phone to Payton.

After a moment of listening to the other end of the line, she responded. "Maxine, this is Payton. Are you free to talk?"

She paused for a moment. "No problem. I'm here at the store. Why don't you give me a call when you can speak? I'll be here until five today...okay... Mm hmm. Thanks."

She hung up and let out a sigh of relief.

"She must be with Jack. She was pretty limited on words, but she said she would try to reach out to me by the end of the day," Payton said.

"Great. Now you can say you've done your part. The rest is on her. Trust me on this... you are going to feel so much better when it's behind you. I would just sit her down woman to woman, and whatever you do, end by letting her know that contacting you in the future can't continue."

"Right. The thing is... she hasn't reached out to me since she came to the store last week," she said.

"It doesn't matter. I took her as the persistent type. One who will wait awhile and then try another tactic. I would just deal with it and then be done," I said, waving it off like it was no big deal.

"Now, enough about that. I need your advice on a few issues that've been plaguing me and Wyatt as of late," I said.

"What's up? Everything all right with you two?"

"The truth. We're struggling." I confessed.

"No. Are you serious? Is it still about the bills?"

"That's precisely what it's about."

"I thought the job here at the shop would help make a difference. Are you guys still coming up short?" Payton asked.

"No, we have everything we need to cover the bills and meet the kids' needs. Everything is paid up to date, trust me. We just don't have a lot to go around after everything is covered. As a result, Wyatt and I are bumping heads more often than not."

"Is there something I can do to help?"

"Payton, believe me, you've already done enough. Giving me this opportunity to come and work at Picture Perfect with you is more than I could ask for. The pay and the flexibility have been amazing. No other job would pay me what you're paying, and we fully recognize and appreciate that. This has everything to do with two people who are frustrated with being in so much debt. It's going to take forever to get back to square one," I said.

"No, it won't. It may be tough at first, but you and Wyatt are strong. You'll see this thing through and come out stronger. I know it's probably not what you want to hear but it's true."

"Payton, we're not even having sex, anymore. We stopped a long time ago. At first I thought it was our schedules getting to us, but now I know. I think there's more to it than that," I responded.

"Do you think he's-"

"Who, Wyatt? Oh, no. He's been working from home. I

don't know when he'd find the time to cheat." The thought gave me such an ill feeling inside. Payton didn't say anything, so I continued.

"Like I said, I feel pretty confident about what he's doing when I'm not around. I honestly think the stress from the debt is weighing in on our marriage," I replied.

"Have you talked to him about it?"

"No."

"Well, Abby, I'm no marriage expert. God knows you've been married much longer than I have, but why don't you go home tonight and talk to the man? Pour a glass of wine after the kids go to bed and sit down and talk."

I gazed out front recalling the last time I tried to have a heart to heart with Wyatt. It felt like he had such a short fuse, always diverting the conversation on to other things. But, maybe Payton was right. Maybe if I offered him a relaxing atmosphere, he'd feel inclined to open up.

"I guess you're right. I mean, the walls of defense have to come down with a nice glass of wine and perhaps some music," I said.

"That's the spirit. Who knows... maybe if you play your cards just right you'll get lucky before the night's over," she said.

"Ha, it used to be the other way around, him wanting to get lucky with me. Believe it or not, my mind isn't even going there. I just want to reconnect with Wyatt, that's all."

"That's definitely a way to reconnect, but I hear what you're saying," she said.

Wyatt and I had always been the best of friends. Way before we ever considered saying I do or having kids. Way before we got into major debt. I didn't want the debt to ruin the very thing that tied us together. Secretly, thoughts lingered in the back of my mind about whether there was another woman of interest, but I wouldn't plant those seeds out loud to Payton or anyone else. Wyatt had never been that type of guy. He had always made me feel like the apple of his eye.

"Abby?"

"Huh? I'm sorry. I got lost in thought there for a second. Did you say something?" I asked.

"Yes, I was wondering if you'd like to tackle the inventory today. We need to submit a few orders and I want to go over a few things you'll need to know while I'm gone."

"Sure."

Later that evening, the kids were in bed and all the evening chores were complete. I wiped down the counters one more time, hoping Wyatt would come out of his office soon. He mostly exchanged conversation with the kids at dinner, asked briefly about my day, and soon returned to take a virtual meeting with one of his clients.

I could hear him shuffling around in his office which I took as a cue that he was off the call.

"Wyatt, do you have a moment?" I said, peering through the door.

"Uh... sure. I was just finishing up with a few odds and ends. How can I help you?" he asked.

I chuckled nervously.

"How can I help you? You sound like you're talking to one of your clients."

He let out a deep, long sigh.

"I meant nothing by it, Abby, honestly. I guess I'm just in work mode, that's all," he said.

"I understand, and I come in peace, really. It's just ten o'clock, and I was hoping we'd have time to talk before I turn in for the night, that's all. It's kind of hard to catch up with you these days."

I didn't mean to sound like I was complaining. In my heart, I just missed my husband.

"It's not intentional. The cases are coming in non-stop and I'm having a hard time balancing the load. They're working on hiring another lawyer soon, hopefully that will help," he responded.

"That makes sense."

There was a quiet lull. One that was recognizable, more often than not.

"That would explain why you don't have as much time to spend with me lately," I said.

"Abby, come on. Don't do this tonight, please." He snapped.

"Don't do what, Wyatt? I'm not trying to do anything but connect with you. Is that too much to ask? Wait... let's stop right now before this gets out of hand. I sincerely came in here to invite you to take a moment to unwind with me. That's all. I have some light music playing out in the living room, and I even poured you a glass of your favorite wine. Sorry, but I didn't know any other way to get your attention but to come in here. If it's a bad time, I'll save it for another night."

The tension in the room relaxed. Wyatt put the paper he was holding on his desk, turned off his lamp, and followed me out to the kitchen.

"Thank you for this. I've been so buried in work lately, I guess it's easy to forget to come up for air," he said.

"I know everything you do is for us, so I try not to complain. But, honey, if you don't take care of yourself, you won't be able to do the job."

"You're right."

"I know it hasn't been easy with the bills and all, but we're in this together. I miss you, Wyatt." I slid his glass across the center island.

"You do?" he asked.

I wondered what would make him ask such a question. There were so many nights I went to bed by myself, longing to have my companion nearby to talk to until we drifted off to sleep.

"I guess it has been a while since we spent quality time together. Although, I figured after a long day at the store and with the kids and all... I just assumed you wouldn't want to be bothered. Plus, I'm almost certain you're pretty unhappy with all the cutbacks we've had to make. Just the other day, I heard you complaining about needing a haircut and a pedicure. I know you're not used to this alternative lifestyle, and it's probably hurting you inside. I'm probably not at the top of your list of favorite people right now, I'm sure."

"Wyatt, why would you say that? Did you forget, I'm just as much to blame for this debt. It's like I said, we're in this together. Plus, you'll always be my number one. I wouldn't trade you in for anyone else. I was just hoping you weren't losing interest in us. I'm the one who was getting a little worried. You used to get so excited about coming to bed with me at night," I said.

He put his glass down and knelt down before me. "Abby,

you have my heart from now until the day I breathe my last breath. I could never and will never lose interest in you. Even if we have to eat Ramen noodles for the rest of our lives." He smiled.

"Get out of here. We're not eating Ramen noodles now, you big goofball."

"I know. But you get where I'm going with this. All I want is to be with you and for us to be happy. I just need to do a better job of not letting the stress of work weigh me down to the point where spending time with my wife becomes nonexistent."

"Thank you, Wyatt. That means a lot to me," I said.

He stood up and kissed me before returning to his glass.

"I know a way that you can make up for the lost time together."

"What do you have in mind?" he asked, nestling close to me.

"We probably should take our glasses upstairs so I can show you." I teased with a flirtatious smile.

"Or... we can sneak around down here in our own house like two young teenagers in love. No one will know but us," he said.

"What if the kids come downstairs?"

He led me to our adult hideaway, a place on the main floor we used to frequent whenever we needed a little mommy and daddy time.

JOLENE

*J*served Will his favorite lunch in the kitchen and prepared sandwiches for Helen and the girls. Today we were having a family meeting to discuss the news of my leaving and the need for all hands on deck to help hire somebody new. Helen made pitchers of lemonade and served the most decorative cookies you ever did see.

"Helen, you sure do have a knack for hosting, even when it's just us girls. Your experience from the hospitality industry paid off in more ways than one," I said.

"Thank you, Jolene. I guess it just comes naturally. Then again, mom was always particular about everything she served. Maybe I picked it up from her. If there was ever a woman who should've had her own hospitality business, she was it. Speaking of hospitality, how's everything at the inn? I haven't heard you say much about it lately."

"Fine, I guess," I replied.

"You guess?"

"I'm sure everything is running smoothly as it always is. It's been a few days since I've been over there, that's all."

I tried to sound casual, but I'm certain it didn't go over so well. The truth was, I hadn't gone back to the inn after my last encounter with David. I figured if I did, I wouldn't know what to say, or where to begin. I dusted off the chairs and pulled up a seat under the umbrella.

"Going to the inn has become such a regular habit for you, I can only imagine how much you're going to miss it once you're gone," Helen said.

"Yes, it's one of the many things I'm going to miss," I said, remembering the way David kissed me.

"Did you tell David?"

"I did. He was a little disappointed, but overall, I know he knows how much this means to me," I said.

"Interesting."

"What?" I asked.

"I just find your version of the story to differ slightly from what I've been hearing around town."

I sat up, giving Helen my undivided attention.

"What did you hear?"

"Well, I'm not saying there's any truth to it, even though I don't see why anyone would make it up, but the word around town is that you and David have been spending a lot of time together. You may see it as a way to pass the time while enjoying an innocent drink at the bar, but apparently, he's into you. That's been going around for some time now. The part I didn't know about was the mouth-to-mouth session you two were having in the garden a few days ago. I heard the poor guy ended up walking away with a broken heart. Is that true?" Helen asked.

Just then Payton, Rebecca, and Abby arrived, sliding the glass door open to join us on the deck. It was poor timing, but I didn't care. I wanted to know where Helen heard all of this information.

"Somebody clearly has too much time on their hands. Was it your nosey friend, Norma Jean who told you this?" I asked.

"Oh good grief, some things never change. Are you two at it again?" Rebecca asked.

"No." Helen giggled as she kissed her daughters hello. "We're not at it. Jolene is just surprised that half the town knows her business, that's all. Pull up a chair and sit down."

Payton made herself comfortable on a nearby lounge chair, while everyone else joined us at the table. The one thing I couldn't stand about living in such a small beach community was everyone poking around in each other's business. At least back home we all had several acres between us. They may have gossiped about whatever they witnessed in town, but I spent most of my time on my land and didn't have to worry about it as much.

"Well, is somebody going to fill us in?" Abby asked.

"No!" I said.

"Oh, Jolene. We're all grown women here. I don't know what the big deal is. You should be allowed to have a personal life that involves a man. It's been a long time since you had someone special around. We get it. Plus, David isn't who I thought he was when Payton and I first met him. We thought for sure he was trying to make a quick buck by purchasing the inn and turning it into some big-time commercial chain hotel. But, he didn't do that. From what I've heard, he's paying careful attention to detail, and he really cares about the people of Pelican Beach. That's all that matters," Helen said.

"You're right, Mom. We judged him too quickly. As a matter of fact I think we all could do a better job of showing our support by going there more often when we're in the mood to dine out. Mom, I'm sure we would incline your friends to follow suit if they see you showing support." Payton added.

"Agreed. I was even going to suggest that Jolene have David back next year for the holidays, but I guess it's too late for that now," she said.

"Why is it too late?" Abby asked.

They directed their attention toward me. It wasn't exactly the intro I was looking for, but one way or another, I had to share the news.

"Well, now that I have your undivided attention... First, I should start by saying, Helen, you had a very crafty way of avoiding my question when I asked who is spreading my business around town. Just know that I haven't forgotten and I plan on revisiting the subject," I said with a smirk.

"As for the rest of you, Helen and I gathered you here over lunch to tell you I'm making plans to return to Jacksonville. To get right down to it, I miss home. I miss my life... as it was. Plus, I think it's time that Will and your mother had someone who can serve as more of-"

"An employee?" Helen interrupted.

"Right. An employee. There's nothing like having healthy boundaries that allow you to maintain a balance between personal and work-life," I said.

"So, who's going to be here for Dad?" Rebecca asked.

"Great question. We're working on it now. It's part of the reason I invited you here. We've always made big decisions like this as a family. Your father isn't able to have as much of a say, but I was hoping we could all put our heads together and see if we can find a nurse's aide to come work with us here at the house. It would have to be someone we could trust, but I think we can make it work," Helen said.

"Also, I've already committed to staying as long as needed. My plans to leave would only happen after the new person is settled in." I reassured them.

"Cousin Jolene, where will you live when you return to Jacksonville?" Payton asked.

I could feel my muscles tensing up. I didn't have the slightest idea. I had hopes of reclaiming my home. I'd saved up a decent amount from what Helen was paying me to try to work out a deal with the bank. It wasn't nearly enough to actually buy the place, but I thought maybe if I could sit down and talk with the branch manager, I could work something out. I guess it was foolish of me to think it could work, but it was my only plan. Unless I could rent out one of the other nearby houses and pick up another job, I was out of luck. I didn't have a Plan B.

"I'm not sure yet. Right now, I'm dedicating my full time and attention to helping Will and Helen for as long as they need me. Then, when the dust has settled, I'll focus on me."

"I'll give it to you. If I had a guy as hot as David pursuing me, I don't know that I could just walk off without at least having a little fun and seeing where it goes." Rebecca teased.

"Rebecca, you hush now. That man is old enough to be your father," Helen replied.

"That means he's experienced. There's nothing like a man who knows what he's doing," she said.

Everyone spilled over into uncontrollable laughter.

"Rebecca, you have a knack for saying what's on your mind. It's something we've always shared in common. It's too bad we haven't spent more quality time together since I've been here," I said, then shifted to address Payton and Abby.

"To all of you... I know you weren't too fond of the idea of me living here with your mother and Will when I first arrived. We didn't exactly get off to a splendid start, but somehow I'd like to think that changed over time. For the remaining time that I'm here and even when I visit in the future, I hope that will change," I said.

"Cousin Jolene, you are one of a kind. You always have been, and that's what makes this family so special. We're all cut from a different mold with our personalities and quirky habits. But, we're family, and we're here for each other. If you need anything... help with the move, or help with finding a place to stay, just say the word and I'll be here." Abby offered.

"That makes two of us," Rebecca said.

Payton patted her belly.

"I don't know how much lifting I can do, but I'll be here for moral support, for sure. Although, I still think you should consider other options. Your heart is in Jacksonville, but your family is here. You can always go back and visit when you get tired of us, but there's nothing like having family nearby to be there for one another. I think we all can attest to that, can't we?" Payton said.

"Are you really that unhappy here in Pelican Beach?" Rebecca asked.

I glanced over at Helen, trying to carefully find the right words.

"Rebecca, I don't know that unhappy is the right word. David reminded me I haven't allowed myself the opportunity to experience all that Pelican Beach offers. My head's been buried in the sand, if you will. Who knows, maybe I would've enjoyed it more," I said.

"It's okay to say what you're really thinking, Jolene. If we're being honest, we both can be generals bumping heads and getting in each other's way. It's not like we don't mean well or love each other... it's just... Jolene needs to make a life for herself. One that doesn't involve working around the family twenty-four hours a day. You girls can understand that, I'm sure," Helen replied.

There was a somber feeling that lingered after we spoke of my plans to leave. I hadn't seen it coming. I always thought everyone learned to tolerate me but had no idea that I'd actually be missed. Will joined us, napping in a nearby chaise lounge. He was present, yet not really in tune with the idea that we were making plans for his care. We spent the next hours tossing around names and nearby institutions for nursing care, each of the ladies leaving with some research to do.

Around eight o'clock I tugged a bar stool out of the way, looking around to see if David was on shift for the night. He owned the place, but no one would know it by the way he blended among the staff, working just as hard as the rest of them. A few women passed by dressed in Hawaiian skirts, wearing leis. Torches were lit and people were dancing by the Veranda.

"What in the heck is going on around here?" I said to the stranger sitting beside me.

"It's their annual Hawaiian themed night. The former owners used to put on a large-scale Hawaiian themed party every year. Folks from the entire beach area would come out and celebrate. The current owner scaled it back a bit, but it's still a nice event. You must not be from around here," the gentleman said.

"I've been living here long enough, but I guess I've been missing out. Besides, I'm a little too old to go around shaking my fanny in a bikini and a two-piece wearing a leis around my neck. Those days are long gone. It's a nice concept for the younger folks, though."

"Ma'am, I don't know you, but from the looks of things, you do not know what you're talking about. I know plenty of men who'd die to see you out there on the dance floor," he said.

Just then David showed up and slipped the man his tab. He was swift and direct, as if he meant to send a message.

"My drawer is short, but if you take the tab over to the other end of the bar to Frank, he'll be able to assist you," he said.

"Sending me on my way so soon? I was just having a pleasant conversation with this fine lady," he said, licking his wet lips and looking at me like I was a piece of prime rib.

He wore shorts, docker shoes, and a floral button-down shirt. His white hair was combed to the side, and he smelled like he bathed in a bottle of old spice. I thought all the extra attention was rather funny, but I don't think David was taking too kindly to it.

"You've had enough for the evening, Phil. Last thing I'd want is for you to pick up a DWI after leaving my place of business. Now, be wise about this and go check out with Frank. If you don't, I'm taking your keys and calling a taxi. Is that what you want?"

He cocked back in the chair before picking up the tab and reading it.

"I guess you're right," he said.

He raised up from the chair and gathered his things. "I don't think I got your name, Miss..."

David slipped a short glass my way.

"Ah, it's probably best you didn't. You have a good night, now. Get home safe." I returned my attention to David, thanking him, and took my first sip.

"So much for the Aloha spirit around these neck of the woods. I'm out of here. Have a good night." He waved his hand and left, sounding disgruntled.

"Thanks for the drink... and for saving me from Phil," I said.

"I wasn't saving you. He needed to get out of here before he reached his drinking limit for the night. If it was just about him hitting on you, I'm sure you could handle yourself just fine."

"Well, excuse me. I just thought since, you know-"

"Since what? Let me guess, you thought since I revealed my feelings and you shut me down, I'd go around acting like a sad puppy with my tail between my legs, vying for your attention?" he said.

"Whoa, whoa, wait a minute. Is that really necessary? I came down here to see you... to talk to you, David. Not to become a target. That's not fair, and if that's the kind of mood you're in, let me know now so I can leave."

He put a bottle of wine on ice and grabbed a few napkins.

"I'm sorry. I didn't mean it the way it sounded," he said without making eye contact.

"Look, I have to deliver this upstairs to one of our honeymoon suites. Enjoy your beverage, and if you want, put in an order for something to eat. I'll be right back."

I watched him until he disappeared out of sight, while thinking about Rebecca's words.

I'll give it to you. If I had a guy as hot as David pursuing me, I don't know that I could just walk off without at least having a little fun and seeing where it goes.

I'm not sure there was much to it, but I was definitely becoming curious about David, maybe even a little torn, or perhaps confused about whether I should stay or go. For now, I was going to let my thoughts stew over a nice steak and the rest of my drink.

PAYTON

$\mathcal{M}$axine was scheduled to arrive within the hour. I was on pins and needles but shifted my attention to everything going on in the shop. Abby was in the back reorganizing the shelves, and our part-time worker, Darlene, was about to finish up with her first day on the job. We didn't spare any time putting her to work with a few clients who needed passport photos and a mother who wanted pictures of her six-month-old.

"Darlene, you did an amazing job today. My clients loved you and I feel so much better knowing the photos will be in the hands of a true professional when I'm gone."

"Thank you, Payton. This was a light day for me. I look forward to returning tomorrow. Nine a.m., correct?" she asked.

"Yes, nine o'clock is perfect. We'll make it another five-hour shift, if that's all right with you?"

"Yes, please. The five-hour shifts give me plenty of time to work on any side jobs I have lined up for the day. I think everything will be just fine when you're on maternity leave. Abby and I get along great. With her running the store and me staying on top of the appointments, everything will run like a well-oiled machine," she said.

"Let's hope so. Abby is a wonderful store manager but every once in a while she comes up with these projects that can be endless." I chuckled.

"I heard that," Abby yelled from the back.

You could hear an aerosol spray can coming all the way from the back room.

"See what I mean," I whispered.

Darlene nodded.

"Don't worry, I'm pretty good at organizing in between photoshoots. We'll be just fine."

"Thank you, Darlene. Well, enjoy the rest of this gorgeous day and I'll see you first thing in the morning." I smiled.

"See you then."

In the back room the shelves used for organizing binders were completely out of place or spread out on the floor. Abby was in the center of it all testing out paint colors.

"Abby, when I said reorganize, I was thinking something simple, like a little light dusting and rearranging the binders," I said as I covered my nose from the awful smell.

"Don't worry. There's a method to my madness. I already went through all the binders. Everything is in order, with maybe a few exceptions. I'm sorry, Payton, but I just had to address these shelves. I was thinking, instead of you purchasing new bookshelves, we could just spruce these babies up with some spray paint. It looks pretty, doesn't it?" she asked, with a can of turquoise paint in hand.

"Lovely. Except there's one problem. The toxic fumes are going to chase the customers away."

"Not to worry. I was just sampling a shelf or two to see if it would be worth my time. I'm going to drag the other shelves out back so I don't stink up the place," she said.

"Great idea. Hey, by the way, Maxine will be here in less than an hour. I was going to have her sit on the couch in the front parlor with me. If you could stay within earshot that would be perfect. You know, just in case I need you for anything. I doubt it, but you never know."

"Uh-"

"What's wrong, Abby? You don't look so hot. I'll bet those fumes are getting to you, aren't they?" I asked.

"Not quite. I think your guest is here a little early. Look behind you, Payton."

I turned around to the sight of a gorgeous woman, about 5'6 standing in heels wearing an a-line sun dress. I remembered her being beautiful, but with her hair all done up and her mascara in place, Maxine was even more stunning than I recalled.

"Maxine, I'm sorry. I didn't hear you come in."

I stood a few feet away, feeling so inadequate.

"No worries. I'm actually here earlier than expected. Jack called and asked me to be ready for some cocktail event at the last minute. It's not for a couple of hours so I thought I'd leave early to give us plenty of time to talk," she responded.

I smiled on the outside. Did she really think I cared to hear about Jack calling or their plans for the evening? *I guess this is what you get when you make plans to speak to your ex-husband's fiancé,* I thought.

Abby waved and returned to the shelves.

"Well, there's no time like the present. My sister is working in the back. You and I can take a seat in the parlor area so we can talk. We shouldn't have many interruptions. It normally gets quiet around this time of day."

"Thank you."

She sat on the couch while checking out the surroundings. I noticed she was sitting on the edge of the couch, patting her dress down a few times. I wasn't sure if the girl was nervous or if the accommodations were beneath her standard. Either way, she didn't look comfortable.

"Can I get you a bottle of water?" I asked.

"No, no. I'm fine, thank you."

"Okay. So, how can I help you?" It was probably a stupid question, but somebody had to get the conversation started.

She turned toward me.

"This is awkward, Payton."

No fooling, I thought.

"There's no nice way to approach the matter so, I'm just going to come right out with it. I was wondering if Jack had a gambling problem when you two were married."

I paused for a moment.

"Gambling or any other addictions that stood out?" She implied.

"Gambling?...no. He was a big spender, but he always told me the money went toward showing his clients a good time, or for his suits and maintaining a certain standard for all things work related. You know how it is."

"Uh huh." She nodded.

"What other addictions are you referring to?" I asked.

She looked around again.

"Addictions with women," she said.

Abby started coughing uncontrollably in the back.

"I'm okay. My soda went down the wrong pipe. Carry on. I'll be outside if you need me," she said.

I took a deep breath.

"Sorry about that. I'm not quite sure what you're referring to, but if you're trying to ask me if he was ever with another woman, I hate to be the one to break it to you, but it's the reason we got a divorce in the first place. I'm sure he was at least up front with you about that, right?"

"No," she responded.

"Well, what did he tell you, then? Wait... don't respond to that. I don't want to know. Look, before this conversation goes any further, you have to know that I'm really uncomfortable with this. Jack is a part of my past, yes, but he has absolutely no place in my present or my future. And I hate to say it like this, but neither do you, Maxine. I only agreed to meet with you today because I felt like if I didn't you would only try to contact me again."

She exhaled.

"I understand the position I put you in by reaching out to you. It has to be just as difficult for you as it is for me. Trust me when I tell you, I thought long and hard about writing that letter to you. A few times I ripped it up and threw it out in the trash, before finally working up the nerve to write another letter and mail it. It's just... I don't have anybody else who can help me with this, Payton. It feels like I've been living in complete isolation, separated from reality. Jack doesn't talk to me much. It's just me all by myself in that house in Connecticut with a man who comes home smelling like booze most nights, if he comes home at all." A tear fell from her eye, which she quickly wiped away.

The endless amount of twirling of her fingers revealed just how nervous she was.

"He has everybody out here fooled, thinking we're such a perfect couple with all the constant schmoozing and wining and dining. I swear it's the stuffiest crowd I've ever been around my entire life... and the only reason I'm out here... the only reason myself or any of the wives are here is because the company's gala is being held toward the end of the conference. If it weren't for that, Jack would've left me behind so he could freely do as he pleases. He's probably already freely helping himself to all the beautiful women, while I'm in the hotel room by myself at night."

I felt horrible for this girl. Disgusted was an understatement. It always amazed me why guys like Jack would want to be married at all if all they really wanted was a life without boundaries.

"Maxine, this is awful. I had no idea that things had gotten this bad, but I guess, why would I? I really don't keep up with his life, anymore. Nor should I. If you're this miserable, may I ask why you're proceeding forward with the engagement?" I asked.

Her next few sentences were jumbled in between sobs as she let the flood gates loose. I couldn't hug her... it was too awkward. I just grabbed a box of tissues nearby and placed them on her lap, hoping that would console her a bit.

After taking several deep breaths, she began speaking again.

"I know this is going to sound pretty pathetic, but I don't have anyone else in my life. I came to this country as an exchange student many years ago. I completed my education, landed a solid job in the city, and then after a couple of years, I met Jack. He's the only person who I formed a genuine connection with after my college friends ran off, got married, and had kids," she said.

"So, you're much younger than me, I would imagine?"

"Oh, yeah, there's probably at least ten or fifteen years between us." Her voice began to trail off. I continued staring at her.

"I'm sorry. I didn't mean anything by it," she said, covering her mouth.

"How long have you and Jack known each other?"

"Don't worry, at first I was concerned, but I did the math, and it was at least a full year after you were divorced," she replied with confidence.

In that moment I realized I was dealing with a baby, fresh out of school, with barely enough years of experience under her belt to know what she was getting into. Sadly, she was looking for love in all the wrong places, and ran right into the hands of Jack, a man incapable of offering true love.

"Mm. Well, this is a doozy, if I may say so myself. If you came here looking for any insight from me into the life Jack was living back then or currently living now, I don't think I can help you. He was just as evasive with me then as he is with you," I said.

She wiped the edge of her eyelids.

"The funny thing is I had already given up hope after I left your store a few days ago. I kept asking myself what I was really hoping to gain from all this. I'm sure many would be inclined to bypass meeting altogether, so I thank you for your generosity," she said.

I glanced toward the coo-coo clock.

"I'm probably inserting my foot in my mouth for what I'm

about to say, but I'll only offer a few words of advice if you want to hear it," I said.

"Yes, please... anything."

"Know your worth," I said directly.

"Excuse me?"

"Know... your... worth! I don't know you very well, but you're worth so much more than this. Every day that passes by with you remaining in this God-awful mess is like you sending a clear message that you don't think you can do any better. Is that what you believe about yourself? You think you can't find anyone better than a low down cheating dog who can't keep his zipper zipped long enough to save his life? You don't need that. Honey, no woman deserves to be with someone like that. Now, you'll have to excuse me for being so forward, but I can only say these things with such passion and conviction because I recognize a part of who I used to be in you. I hung in there for a long time, at first in complete denial, then hopeful to the point of becoming hopeless. The whole time the writing was on the wall, just as clear as day. The signs were everywhere, the flags were flying at full staff... but the real question was whether I was willing to pay attention and adhere to what I already knew."

"Well, clearly you did or else you wouldn't be here," she said.

"I did eventually, but I wasted a lot of time feeling so ashamed to come back home to my family and explain what I was going through. To keep it one hundred percent real with you, I did all the wrong things before I finally learned to focus on my worth," I said, lowering my voice.

"There were times when I made myself look as sexy as I possibly could, thinking, maybe, that would help me to win

Jack's love. The only thing I won was a deeper sense of emptiness on the inside. Is that how you want to spend the next ten to fifteen years of your life? Empty and lonely?"

"No," she said, hanging her head low.

"Well, all right then. It's time you figure out what you're going to do about it. That decision is entirely up to you... but respectfully... it shouldn't involve me."

"You're right, Payton. You are one hundred and ten percent correct. It shouldn't involve you, but I can't pretend that coming here wasn't helpful for me. I feel so encouraged after speaking to you. I know what I'm going to do now. I'm leaving Jack. I'm going to march right back to that hotel and let him have it," she said.

"Whoa, slow down there," I said.

The back door slammed shut as Abby returned, ushering in the smell of fresh paint.

"You just said I need to know my worth. So, I'm going to let him know I'm not putting up with his crap, anymore. The engagement is off," Maxine said in a high-pitched voice.

Abby peered around the corner with her eyebrows perched up. I couldn't even begin to explain this one, so instead signaled that everything was okay.

"Maxine, you might want to think this through. After all, you're miles away from home, among his people, not yours."

"Oh, yeah, good point," she responded.

It was all I could do not to roll my eyes at how naïve she was.

I inched toward the edge of the couch and stood up.

"Sorry, it seems like I can't comfortably stay in one position for too long. My lower back is giving me an absolute fit today," I said.

"Please, don't say another word. You've already taken enough time out of your day."

Maxine was still talking, but all I could seem to focus on was my back and the cramp-like feeling that was probing my lower abdomen. Thankfully, my discomfort served as a signal for our meeting to conclude.

JOLENE

"David, we need to talk," I said, demanding his attention. Waiting for him to look me in the eye.

It was obvious he was trying to keep busy.

"It felt good to come here last night and have a drink and dine, like old times. But we still haven't talked to each other since... you know. We can't continue avoiding the pink elephant in the room," I whispered.

"There's no pink elephant, Jolene. Perhaps, you have something you want to get off your chest. If so, I'll listen," he said.

"Do you really want to do this here in front of your customers? Smack dab in the middle of the lunchtime rush?" I asked.

He looked around and called Frank over to cover his spot.

"Why are you always covering this bar, anyway? As the owner shouldn't you be out and about mingling among the guests?" I asked.

"I need to hire someone to help at the bar, but until I do,

this is the area that can get me in the most amount of trouble if I'm not keeping a close eye on things. Don't you worry about how I'm running the inn. I have about ten minutes to spare. Go around through the main entrance and meet me in my office," he said, throwing his towel over his shoulder.

I acknowledged Frank, figuring he was probably wondering what was going on. A quick stroll through the Veranda led me to the main lobby of the inn. The inside looked nothing like I remembered. It was a romantic hideaway, one of Pelican Beach's best-kept secrets... or at least it was to me.

The offices were still positioned in the back across from the conference room. I tapped on the door.

"It's open," he yelled.

Inside, David was flipping through a few papers.

"Certainly, you can't be busy after I just asked you to talk with me?"

"No, I'm not busy, just fiddling around, that's all," he responded.

"Okay, while you're fiddling, would you mind helping me to break the ice between us, please?"

"Jolene, I told you-"

"Never mind what you told me. Your actions speak volumes. I came here last night to clear the air and make sure everything was good between us," I said.

"And, I responded by offering you a meal. I even talked to you. What more do you want, Jolene? It's not easy getting back on your feet after you've been sucker punched, you know."

"David, that's ridiculous. I didn't punch you."

"You punched my ego," he said.

I inched closer to touch his arm.

"That's exactly why I wanted to talk. I didn't mean to

bruise your ego. You just threw me off guard. I didn't know how to respond to you, and I still don't. But, I know one thing for sure. I miss my best friend. I've been the closest to you practically the entire time I've been out here. Wouldn't you rather spend the remaining time I have here enjoying one another like we used to?" I asked.

"No. It may be selfish but that's not what I want."

"Okay. Tell me how you really feel," I said.

He gave me a look out of the corner of his eye.

"Be careful what you ask for," he said.

"I'm serious."

"Jolene, I don't think you are. Matter of fact, I don't think you know what you want."

I nodded. "There's probably some truth to that," I said.

"I know there is, but I can help change that. Why don't you give me a week." He removed his hat and placed it on his desk.

"A week for what?"

"To show you things you've never seen before. A week to help change your mind," he said.

"Are we talking about us or changing my mind about staying here in Pelican Beach?"

"Both. There's only one exception," he said, moving close enough for me to feel his breath.

"And that is?"

"I need you to be totally open with me, willing to experience whatever the week may bring, without reservation," he said.

"I can't promise without knowing-"

"Jolene."

"Yes?"

"This could end up being the best week you've ever had.

Why decide to spoil it before giving it a chance? What are you afraid of?" he asked.

I drew in the scent of his cologne as he placed his lips on the side of my neck, once, twice, several times. Instead of pushing him away, I allowed him to continue. His hand ran slowly up my back, making me feel like a woman all over.

"One week?" I whispered.

"That's right, and if by the end of the week you still view me as only a friend, and Pelican Beach as a place that belongs in your past, then so be it. I'll take it like a man, knowing I gave it my all."

"David, what is one week going to prove?"

"It may prove absolutely nothing, or it may reveal everything you've been missing in your life. There's only one way to find out. The only thing I need to know is, are you in?" he asked.

My mind fantasized about the many ways this could go, both good and bad.

"Jolene... You can't deny that electric current that flows between us when we get this close. I love having you as a friend, but I want more. I want all of you."

"Fine. Kiss me then. I have to hurry up and get back to the house. Give me a pleasant distraction to hold me over until later on this evening." I teased, sounding half sassy and half serious.

He backed off and chuckled under his breath.

"That's not the way this works. What I'm offering is for keeps. I don't think you're taking me seriously. But, that's okay. You'll see."

He adjusted his hat, tipping it in my direction before heading to the door.

"I'll pick you up tonight, let's say around eight, at your place."

"My place? Wait. That's it? You're just going to walk out of here while we're still in the middle of a conversation?"

He took off his hat and returned, kissing me long enough to make me feel light-headed and flush in the face. He kissed me the same way you would an intimate lover you'd been with your entire life.

"Oh, dear. David, maybe I should follow you and grab a quick brandy on the way out."

"Not tonight. Tonight, it's just me and you. No aids, no numbing your feelings."

Placing his hat back on, he pecked me one last time and left me standing in his office.

"Helen, can we talk?" I asked while preparing Will's five o'clock meal.

"Jolene, when have you ever asked to speak to me? I swear lately it's almost as if you're changing right before my very eyes. What ever happened to the bold and outspoken Jolene. Does she still exist?"

I smiled.

"Yes, I'm still here. I've just been so distracted lately."

"By what?" she asked.

"A little bit of everything, I guess. Have you ever felt so lost and confused... not knowing which way to turn next?"

"Oh, hell. Have you been drinking again, Jolene?" she asked.

I chuckled.

"No! I haven't had anything to drink today, and I don't plan on having anything."

"Really? Are you sick?" she asked.

"Helen, will you quit!"

"There she is. There's the feisty Jolene we've all come to know and love. Okay, carry on."

I gave Helen a sideways look for playing around so much.

"As I was saying, I don't know what's wrong with me, but something is not right."

"Why don't you start by being more specific? Are you speaking about moving back to Jacksonville?"

"Yes, that's part of it. I'm just going to lay everything on the table. I put in a call to an old neighbor of mine, and well, things aren't looking too good as far as moving back to where I want to be," I said.

"Okay, well, I'm sure there are other options... right?"

"Maybe. I don't know. I didn't look into other options, yet." I stopped to check her facial expression, which was completely blank.

"You don't expect to move back home without doing any research do you? Surely, you didn't have your heart set on just one place?" she asked.

I turned the front burner off and stared out the window at the point where the ocean line met the sand.

"Jolene, I'm sure you can call a few more people. Perhaps even put in a call to some of the apartment complexes in the surrounding area," Helen said.

"Apartment? Helen, no apartment will compare to my home. The place where I once lived happily with George, and all of our memories together."

"Your home? Wait. Is that what this is about, Jolene? Did

you think by returning to Jacksonville you'd be able to move back into your old house?" she asked.

I opened the oven and pulled out a rack of lamb, prepared just the way Will liked it.

"I was hoping I could," I said. I continued fixing the food without making eye contact.

"How could that be possible when you walked away from the place, leaving it for the bank to take over?"

"I only did it because I got myself into a pinch and needed a little relief. I was hoping I could call the bank and work something out. You know, maybe set up a few installment payments or one of those lease-to-own options. It's not like we had a lot left on the mortgage," I replied.

"Jolene... that's not how these things work. Once the bank takes over, it's theirs to do with as they please. In most cases they look to sell the property to help recoup their loss. They wouldn't entertain making a deal with the same person who couldn't afford-"

She stopped mid-sentence.

"Go ahead, you can say it. I couldn't afford to stay there to begin with. I guess it doesn't matter anyway, because another couple bought the place and recently moved in. Any efforts I would've made would've been for naught."

Helen brought over a pre-mixed salad bowl from the fridge.

"I'm sorry, Jolene. I didn't mean any harm. I know how much the house and the memories of George meant to you."

"Thank you. I packed a lot of those memories up in storage with the rest of my things. It was probably foolish of me to create such a plan in my mind," I said.

"You're probably just missing George. It's understandable."

"I'll always miss him, Helen. But, that's not the reason I

called to inquire about the house. I think I just missed the comfort of being in my home. That was the last place where I felt free to be me. One hundred and ten percent me... Jolene Ferguson... without conforming to somebody else's way of living. No harm intended. It's just the first place that came to mind that was familiar, that's all. I shouldn't have gotten my hopes up."

Feeling a little nervous, I continued sharing.

"The other thing that's been on my mind, which may come as a shock to you, is David," I said.

The corners of Helen's mouth curled into a smile.

"Really? Well, it's nice to finally hear you admit it," she said.

"Admit what?"

"That you like him, that's what. You don't think I've noticed the daily lunch breaks and evenings spent at the inn? *I'm heading over to the inn, I'll be right back... or I'm stopping at the inn on my way to the grocery store... do you need anything?*" Helen mimicked.

"We're good friends. What's the big deal?" I asked.

"You're the one who brought him up, so you tell me. Have you two nestled up next to each other in one of the comfort suites, yet?" she asked with a devilish smile.

"Helen!"

"Come on, spill the tea. You two are meeting for midday rendezvouses, aren't you? I'll bet he makes you feel like a young woman again, doesn't he?"

"Well, he does make me feel alive. But, that's beside the point."

"I knew it! I knew it... I knew it... I knew it," she said.

"You know nothing, Helen. Trust me, it's not what you're

thinking. We're not as far along as you'd like to imagine. Mostly we talk at the bar and that's it. Occasionally, he orders a meal for me, we talk for a little while, and then I come back here to the house. End of story."

"If that's the case, then what did he do to make you feel so alive?" she asked suspiciously.

I relaxed against the counter, fiddling with the dish towel.

"He kissed me in a way that woke up every part of my body and I enjoyed it."

"Whoa, hot momma! That's strike two. The first kiss may have been out of curiosity, but twice... it sounds like he's more than just a friend." Helen teased.

"I knew something was going on." She added.

"That's because of your nosey neighbors, which you still haven't said a word about who's going around spreading my business. Don't think that I forgot to bring it up again."

"Jolene, the only one spreading your business is you. What do you expect to happen when you put on such a public display for a small town to see?"

"Well, this time there was no public display. We went into his office to have a little privacy." As soon as the words came out of my mouth, I realized how terrible it sounded.

"Ooh, his office. Let me guess, did he clear off his desk so you could-"

"No, he did not. If you don't quit teasing me, I won't say another word." I threatened.

"And keep all this to yourself? No way. You've been itching to tell somebody. I'm your best bet outside of talking to David directly," she said.

"Helen, I'm telling you the truth. Nothing happened outside of the kiss, but he did reveal that he wants more than a friendship. I can't seem to wrap my head around it. I'm older than him."

"Do you know that for a fact, or are you just guessing?" she asked.

"We briefly touched on the subject before. It's a guess, but I'll bet a pretty darn good one. Plus, he's traveled the world, owned many businesses, and met a lot of women. What would he want with someone like me?"

"Jolene, don't sell yourself short. You act like an old grump most times, but you have a lot of life left in you. You're an attractive woman and beneath all the nonsense you're constantly spewing out of your mouth, there's a kind soul... deep down in there somewhere." Helen smiled.

I swatted the dish cloth at her and returned to finishing up Will's plate.

"Was that supposed to be a compliment? If so, thanks. I really feel better about myself now." I laughed.

"I'm glad. I'll send your bill in the mail for my services."

"I ought to do more than slap you with a dish towel." I teased.

"Seriously, Jolene. What are you going to do? It seems like you have a lot to think about. Starting up a relationship right now might be a little tricky. Not impossible, but tricky."

"It gets worse."

"I don't know that I can handle much more," Helen replied.

"He asked me to give him a week..."

"A week? For what?" she asked.

"One week to see how I really feel about him... and one week to convince me to stay in Pelican Beach. He said if I'm not convinced, then he'll back off and leave me alone. He's supposed to come by and pick me up tonight around eight. I agreed to it, but I'm not sure it was the right thing to do."

"A week, eh? He sounds pretty confident. He must have serious feelings for you if he's going to such great lengths," she said.

"That's what I'm afraid of. I have to say, Helen, I didn't see this coming."

"Is that such a bad thing? I guess another approach is considering what do you really have to lose? Go out with the guy. Live a little. Wasn't that your biggest complaint? You didn't have a life of your own is what you said... now here's an opportunity at life. Have fun and stop overthinking everything."

"Are you playing devil's advocate? That's easier said than done. I'm supposed to be focused on helping you find a replacement and planning where I'm going to live." I sighed.

"Jolene, did it ever occur to you that this may be the kind of interruption you need? The more I consider this, I'm with David. Worst case scenario, you realize you had a fun week but you two are really meant to be friends and nothing more. Then you can get back to your planning."

"Helen, this is ridiculous." I complained.

"If it's so ridiculous, why didn't you pull away when he kissed you?"

I folded a couple of napkins and placed Will's plate on the table. She was probably right, but I didn't have to admit it.

"Helen, I tried asking myself the same question. The only thing I could think of is how long it's been since I felt the firm hands of a man running down my back."

"Are you sure all you did was kiss?" she asked.

"Yes... yes... that's all we did."

Helen filled a glass with ice and poured Will's drink. Then she walked over and looked me in the eye.

"It's all right to focus on Jolene, you know. You have permission to put yourself first. Even if this turns out to be nothing and you pack everything and go back home. You still deserve the chance to have fun and do something for yourself. If you want to figure your life out, you have to start somewhere, wouldn't you agree?" she asked.

"Since when did you become so good at giving advice? You almost sound like a therapist." I laughed.

"Ha, who knows? Maybe I was one in a former life. Or maybe experience has been a wonderful teacher. Either way, I think what you really need to do is turn the kitchen over to me for the rest of the evening. In just a few hours, your date will be here. Go on upstairs and get ready for him. Borrow something from my jewelry box to wear around your neck, and whatever you do, don't come down here wearing those frumpy old Bermuda shorts. Put on something flattering." She whacked me on the fanny with a wooden spoon.

We both laughed so hard, I stopped and held my legs together to keep from losing control. It felt like we were back to our old selves, enjoying each other like we did when we were younger. I missed that.

JOLENE

"Where are we?" I said, as we pulled up to a discrete area looking over Pelican Beach.

"You've never been to Lookout Point?" David asked.

"No, you have to remember I'm not from around here. Even though I can see why they refer to it as Lookout Point. The stars are absolutely gorgeous. Oh, and there's the beach over there, and if I'm not mistaken, that even looks like the inn over in that direction. Am I right?" I asked.

"Yes, ma'am," he said, while letting down the top to his convertible.

"This is by far one of the best locations in Pelican Beach, outside of the beach itself. Typically, during the weekends this place is filled with young lovers in search of the perfect view, but tonight it's rather quiet. Looks like we picked a good evening to sit back and enjoy," he said.

"How do you know about what goes on up here? Do you come here frequently with other women?"

"No, Jolene. One of my customers mentioned this place a while back as being known for its scenic views. I drove over one day looking for a little break from the inn and I've been hooked ever since. It's not only for lovers, you know. Families come up here with their kids and the tourists do as well."

Leaning back on the headrest allowed for the perfect view of a shooting star. A few of the beach houses in the distance were lit. I tried one by one to find Will and Helen's cottage. But I couldn't so I glanced over toward David instead.

"Thank you for bringing me here. This is a nice treat... and a nice reminder of how I need to get out more," I said.

"I thought you might enjoy it here. This is a lot better than sitting at the bar, isn't it?"

I closed my eyes for a moment and then asked him, "You don't like it when I drink, do you?"

"I didn't say that," he replied.

"You didn't have to. I can detect it."

"I don't have a problem with you having a drink or two. Lots of people use it as a way of helping them to unwind," he said.

"But..." I responded.

"But there is a difference between having a glass to help you unwind versus drinking to mask one's feelings. Sometimes I think you vacillate between the two." He continued.

"Touché. You may know me a little better than I thought."

"Thank you, however, I've also been in the hospitality business for a long time. I've met so many over the years looking for someone who will take the time to listen as they talk about their problems... usually over a glass of something soothing," he said.

"You've been listening to me for a while now. What problems do you think I have besides the obvious problem of wanting to go back home?"

He reclined his seat slightly and let out a soft chuckle.

"I'm entering this conversation with caution. I don't want it to backfire on me." He laughed.

"Don't worry. It won't." I reassured him.

"Well, in that case, I'll just be blunt, then. I think you're misguided."

"Whoa. Slow down there. I didn't say you had free rein to attack me." I teased.

"Listen, do you want to hear the truth or not?"

"Go ahead," I said, rolling my eyes and fixing my hands comfortably over my purse.

"The only reason I say misguided is because you think going home will solve your problems, but it won't. I'll bet money that you'll get unpacked, settle in, only to find that you're still just as unhappy as ever."

My mouth dropped open. He knew nothing about my life back home except for what I shared. I wondered what made him feel so confident to say such a thing.

"Don't look so surprised, Jolene. Come here. Give me your hand," he said, extending his hand over to mine.

"I'm fine. You can continue, I can't wait to hear what else you think about me."

"Joleeennne. Give me your hand, will you?"

I slowly met his hand halfway.

"You know me well enough to know that I don't mean any harm. I care about you."

He covered my hand with his and continued.

"I think you're ready for love again. I think you like being around the family, but you want a life of your own again... a life that includes coming home to your own man at the end of a long day. A life that includes taking care of your own home affairs and not just Helen's all the time. Yeah, sure, you two bump heads but that's not your real issue. At the core of everything you've ever shared with me, I hear a woman who's running away and searching for comfort in what she once had."

"What makes you say a thing like that?"

"The moment you and I start laughing and talking, you forget about home and just enjoy the comfort of being together. The first time I ever touched you at the inn you practically gave way to everything and melted into my arms... then there's today. The same thing occurred... you leaned into me, Jolene... you leaned in like you wanted more. Whether or not you want to admit it, you enjoy what we have together. It's like you look forward to it... every day... and so do I."

He waited patiently for me to reply.

"Well, I don't know what to say. I certainly didn't expect all this. I guess I need to be more conscious of the things I say when I'm talking to you," I said.

"I hope that's not your takeaway from this conversation. That's not what I'm saying at all."

"What are you saying, David? Do you even really know?"

He tapped the steering wheel without providing an answer. Then he flicked the headlights on, turned on the music, and got out of the car.

"What are you doing?" I asked.

"I am not allowing myself to get derailed from the reason I came here tonight."

He left his hat in the driver's seat and walked around to my side of the car, opening the door.

"I didn't come here to argue with you tonight. That's a

waste of time. If anything I said offended you, then I apologize. Since we're here and the night is still young, will you dance with me?"

"Oh, David, I haven't danced in so long, I'd probably step all over your feet." I grumbled.

"There's only one way to find out."

He stood there patiently, waiting for me until I gave in. I grabbed hold of his hand and followed him to the front of the car, carefully navigating the graveled pavement. The warm breeze and the way he began with a gentle sway felt mesmerizing.

"David," I whispered.

"Am I moving too fast?" he asked.

"No, I'm not that old for goodness' sake. I have to ask you something."

"Okay. Fire away."

Without hesitation I asked, "Why me? What is it you see in me? I'm older than you. For as long as you've known me all I ever do is grumble and complain, I'm not established here in Pelican Beach. Why me?" I asked, searching his eyes for an honest answer.

"You're my best friend, Jolene. Why not you? Why can't a guy fall for his sassy, hot-tempered friend? Are there any rules against it?" He chuckled hard at his own response.

"You think you're funny, don't you?" I said, holding up my fists.

"No, all jokes aside. I wasn't looking for it to happen. When we met, I had my head in the sand, buried knee deep in the business. But, you drew me in. You forced me to slow down and pay attention to you. Plus, you were an ear when I needed

someone to listen to me. If you spend enough time with someone, it is possible to grow fond of them, you know."

"Mm hmm." I mumbled.

"And to me... age doesn't matter. When I look at you, I see a
beautiful, vivacious woman that I've been longing to be with
for quite some time now."

"Really?" I asked.

"Ha, you have no idea."

I pondered over what he was saying.

"You mean, you've thought about making love to me?" I asked.

"Yes, Jolene. I'm a man and I do have a pulse, you know."

"I know, but-"

"Look. I don't want to get sidetracked tonight. I'm a
gentleman first and foremost, and I brought you here to give
you a taste of what you've been missing. Pelican Beach is a
wonderful place, Jolene. I think you should give it another
chance before you consider leaving. And, I mean that sincerely
whether you have feelings for me or not," he said.

"I'd be a fool not to admit that I'm attracted to you," I
responded.

I placed my hand on his chest and continued swaying
with him.

"I even like the way it feels, being in your arms. But, I'm not
sure-"

"Shhh," he said, placing his finger over my lips.

"I'm not looking for a response right now. Just dance with
me and take in the beautiful view," he said.

We swayed a little longer, listening to country music and
the sound of the crickets. It was amazing to me that all this time
I viewed David as my bar buddy, my sounding board when I

needed to vent, the entire time never knowing he saw so much more in me.

"Can I say one thing?" I asked.

"Sure."

"I think you are right about me looking for comfort in all the wrong places."

"Well, I didn't quite say it like that, Jolene."

"But, it's how you meant it. There's no harm in calling it like it is. My problem is knowing what comfort is, anymore. Ever since George passed, and then I lost our home, I feel like the last several years of my life have been one big eviction notice. Without me ever having a say so, all the things that mattered to me most were taken away."

He stopped and held me by the shoulders.

"Jolene, the mere fact that you can identify that now is progress. It's a beautiful thing to have that level of understanding. I'll bet it's been tormenting you for a long time," he said.

I laughed.

"For once, I'm actually having an epiphany without a glass of brandy. I better write this down. This is a day to remember." I continued laughing.

"I'll bet there's so much more to discover about yourself if you stop hiding behind the glass. It's just a way to numb your pain, but it doesn't really solve anything," he said.

"True. But, I'm getting better at it. At least better than I was when I first arrived."

When the song ended, David took me by the hand and walked over to the area for sightseeing. Besides one other parked car with a couple inside, it was just us underneath the stars, looking over Pelican Beach.

"David," I whispered.

"Yes," he whispered in return.

"Kiss me again, and this time don't hold anything back."

"Right here with the headlights shining on us?" he asked.

I glanced around, thinking about it for a moment.

"No, perhaps somewhere more intimate. Maybe we can go back to the inn." I suggested.

"I don't know if that's a good idea. I'm not a replacement for the things you're longing for, Jolene. George... your home-town... I can't give you those things. You can spend the night with me out of desire or mere curiosity and still wake up feeling just as empty. If you spend any time at the inn with me, I want it to be because you truly want to be with me. My feelings for you are real. Please, don't experiment with my heart."

"That's not my intention. But, I have desires and it's your fault they've been awakened. Kiss me, David."

We spent the next several minutes locked in each other's arms. We freely explored what it was like to cross the lines of friendship into something more. At that moment I knew I was in trouble. I was making it even harder to decide about my future.

PAYTON

My c-section wasn't scheduled for another week, and for the first time I was afraid to take any chances by being at work. I left the store yesterday feeling satisfied about bringing closure to things with Maxine. I then called the doctor to explain my symptoms, but since they quickly subsided, he ordered me to go home, rest, and scolded me for being at the store to begin with.

Tonight, Cole laid beside me watching t.v. while I positioned myself on my lazy boy pillow.

"How are you feeling, honey?" he asked, while flipping through the channels.

"No different than I did about an hour ago. I've given up on the idea of laying down in a comfortable position. It will just be me, my pillow, and this magazine until I eventually nod off to sleep tonight."

"I'm here with you, but I can't imagine your neck is going to feel too good in the morning. Last night you were bobbing and weaving like crazy," he said.

"Yeah, well, there's not much else I can do about it. I continuously remind myself that it's only one more week. If I made it this far, then my neck, back, and every other part of me can hang in there for one more week. Oh, and did I forget to mention, after this I'm getting my tubes tied?" I teased.

"Wow, how did we go from trying to find a way to be comfortable to tying tubes?"

"I'm messing with you, Cole. However, we're definitely not getting any younger. It might not be a bad idea."

"Perhaps, but I have another theory as to why your body may have gone into a little distress yesterday," he said.

"I already know what you're going to say."

"Well, humor me, anyway. It's no coincidence that all this happened on the same day you met with Maxine. All I want to know is that you're one hundred and ten percent confident that woman is going to leave you alone now that you had your little talk," he said.

"I'm pretty sure of it. Even though I have to admit I feel kind of sorry for the girl. Jack is only with her because she's a hot, young, pretty thing... What do they call it? Eye candy? That's what she is in his eyes. A nice-looking woman to have on his arms. He doesn't really love her the way she deserves to be loved. He's been getting away with doing whatever he wants because she's been too afraid to tell him to kick rocks," I said with my mouth curled up in disgust.

"Hold on, now. Our aim is to keep you calm. Whatever Jack has going on has nothing to do with us. I just hope all parties are satisfied and we can put all this behind us. You know I love you, but I can't be as supportive if she comes around again. I'm sorry," Cole said.

"You're so protective, honey. I love it when you stand up for me. It's sexy," I said, pinching his cheek.

"Ha... ha... ha... very funny, Payton. I'm serious. Me, Emmie, and the twins deserve to have you to ourselves. Let's let the past be in the past, where it belongs."

He laid across my lap, looking up at me with puppy dog eyes and kissed my belly.

"I'm not making fun of you. I'm serious when I say I think it's sexy when you're protective. I also agree it's time we close that chapter of our lives and move on," I said.

"We should celebrate our future," he said, springing up from the bed.

"Uh, okay."

"Do you realize we are a week away from one of the most exciting milestones in our lives since the day we said I do?" he asked.

I giggled.

"Cole, I'm reminded every single day. The babies are still inside, jabbing me as we speak."

"That's because they're excited, too. I'll be right back. I'm going to go downstairs and grab some sparkling apple cider, or water, or anything non-alcoholic so we can make a toast."

"I'll bet Emmie is still up. Why don't you grab her and see if the two of you can whip up one of her brownie sundaes while you're at it?" I yelled. Cole was already out the bedroom door, excited like a kid in a candy shop.

~

"Oh my God, Cole, wake up," I said, nudging him on his arm.

He shot up, screaming something about the burglar alarm. I don't know what he was dreaming about, but now was not the time for a delirious performance.

The clock displayed three-thirty a.m.

"Cole, wake up. Something doesn't feel right." I repeated.

"Oh, man. I literally thought I heard the alarm sounding off in my sleep. I was having the craziest dream. There was this guy-"

"Cole! I said something feels abnormal."

I stood up, hoping that going to the restroom would help make a difference. That's when I was overwhelmed with a warm sensation saturating my legs and the floor beneath me.

"Uh... Doc may have misread this one. My water just broke," I said.

"Your water just broke? Wait, what?"

"Cole, go into the bathroom and splash some water on your face. We need you to be alert so we can get to the hospital a.s.a.p.," I said, trying to remain calm.

"I'm on it. I'll help you downstairs, wake up Emmie, and grab your overnight bag. Or maybe I should start by getting dressed first, then I can help with the-"

"Cole! Get dressed!" I yelled, hoping to snap him out of his delirious state.

Emmie knocked on the door and peered into the room.

"I heard somebody yell. Is everything okay?" she asked.

"Everything is going to be fine. Payton is in labor. You remember what we practiced, right?"

"Yeah."

"Good. Go put it into action. Get dressed, grab your bags, and we'll meet you downstairs in five minutes."

Emmie disappeared.

I dialed doc's emergency line to let him know we were on our way. Afterward, I cleaned up as best I could and threw on a comfortable maxi dress. Cole, on the other hand, was fumbling around in his closet. At the point in which I saw a sock fly across the room, it occurred to me he may have been a tad bit more nervous than me.

"Cole. Are you finding everything okay?" I asked.

"I'm putting on my sweats. No worries, I'll be right there."

"Good, because these contractions are starting to ramp up. I'm trying to stay calm but at the rate things are moving along, I just don't know."

He emerged from the closet with his hair looking disheveled.

"Don't worry, I've got this under control," he said.

With help from Emmie, we were in the car in no time. Every bump along the road caused me to hold my belly, bracing and gripping the door, in readiness for the next contraction. I can recall looking out the window praying for help to get through this, wishing the hardest part was over.

"Emmie, how are you doing back there?" I asked in between calculated breaths.

"I'm good, but I'm not the one who's in labor. I should be asking how you are doing?"

"Aww, sweet girl. I'll be all right. I'm trying to keep my mind occupied with good thoughts. Listen, once we get to the hospital your dad will make arrangements for Aunt Abby to come pick you up."

"Okay," she responded.

"I want you to help her out at the store if she needs it, and in a couple of days when I come home, I'll need you to be ready for us. It's going to be all hands on deck."

"Got it. I know I'm still really young, but after seeing you like this, I think I might decide to adopt children instead."

Cole laughed before clearing his throat and holding my hand.

"I'm sure by then you'll have a change of heart, Emms. The reward on the other side is worth it. Just wait until you meet your sisters, you'll see what I mean."

The ride to the hospital was the longest fifteen minutes of my life. Nevertheless, we made it and now it was time for the real adventure to begin.

Later that morning, after an emergency c-section, and Cole nearly passing out with his nerves working in overdrive, our two healthy baby girls were born. Ella arrived first, weighing almost six pounds, and Elizabeth slightly less. Mom was the first family member to arrive and meet them for the first time.

"Oh my heavens, the twins are absolutely beautiful. Look at those plump, rosy cheeks," she said as she held their little fingers.

"Payton, I am so proud of you. The doctor told me you walked in the hospital like a trooper, ready to dive into action. He also said that a small percentage of women go into labor before a planned c-section... I guess you fit the description," she said.

"I guess so. All I can remember is making it from the car, into a wheelchair, and next thing you know they were prepping Cole and getting him into his scrubs. He's the real trooper for not passing out in the operating room."

"Oh, boy, I don't think I'm ever going to hear the end of this one, am I?" he asked.

"Nope, probably not."

Mom continued cooing over the girls. She inspected them carefully, identifying ways to tell them apart.

"I'm just sorry we couldn't carry on with our usual tradition of having the entire family here to welcome these precious little girls, but the hospital has their rules. Jolene dropped me off and you know your father would be here if he could, but we thought it was best that he stay at the house and meet the twins when they come home," she said.

"I understand, Mom. The doctors are just taking extra precautions because it was a c-section, that's all. All everyone talks about is making sure I take it easy and not overdo it after having such a major surgery."

"Of course, dear. Oh, before I forget, Abby called and said she would bring Emmie by after the store closes this afternoon," she said.

"Thank you, Helen. My mom is going to swing by and pick up Emmie before then. I know she's excited to meet the twins," Cole said.

"Okay, I'll let her know. Also, Rebecca will be here within the hour. The nurse told me you could have two visitors, but you feel free to kick us out any time you're ready. I know you must be tired."

"Honestly, the only thing I feel is pure joy, right now. I must be on an adrenaline high. I just can't believe these two, precious, little human beings belong to me." I smiled.

Just then Nurse Jenson walked in.

"Well, believe it, honey... and just in case you need a reminder, you'll have all the diapers, grocery bills, college tuition, birthday celebrations, first car, and everything in between to remind you. Your pockets won't let you forget!" Nurse Jenson chuckled.

"How's momma and her sweet babies doing?"

"I think we're all a little drowsy, but that's to be expected," I responded.

"Good. I'm just going to take your temperature. It will be quick."

She looked over at Cole as he nestled in a chair beside my bed.

"Dad, how are you holding up over there?"

"Pretty good considering how lightheaded I was earlier." He laughed.

"Did you say you have a daughter at home who's in middle school?"

"I sure do, and I already know where you're going with this, Nurse Jenson. Yes, I have experience with labor and delivery, but I was a chicken then and apparently, I'm still one now," Cole said, making fun of himself.

"That's funny, you never mentioned a thing about it to me."

"I was hoping I'd conquer my labor room jitters this time around. Guess I still have some work to do," he said.

We all laughed. I put his mind at ease by reminding him that we wouldn't be returning any time soon.

"Well, either way, you hung in there and that's what matters most," Nurse Jenson said.

"Thank you. Honestly, we owe a big thank you to you and the nursing team. You guys have been nothing short of amazing," Cole said.

"Aww, thank you. That's what we're here for."

She removed the thermometer from my mouth, appearing satisfied with the results.

"Nurse Jenson, I was wondering something," I said.

"Sure, ask away."

"I have a father at home who's in need of a full-time nurse's aide to help provide care for him. He has dementia, and my mother could use an extra pair of hands to help with his care. Do you know of anyone who might be available or perhaps an agency you could recommend?" I asked. Mom's eyes lit up at the idea.

"I don't know of anyone, but I can certainly ask around for you. The nurses look out for each other around here. If anyone is looking for a job, you'll be one of the first to know."

"That would be wonderful." Mom added.

"I'll start asking around today. In the meantime, it looks like sweet Elizabeth is ready to eat. Mom, I hope you're ready to start putting some of those breastfeeding techniques we talked about into practice."

"Yes, ma'am. I'm as ready as I'll ever be."

JOLENE

$\mathcal{I}$ brought Helen home from the hospital in time to have lunch with William. Afterward, I visited with Payton for a little while, waiting patiently for a turn to meet the twins. It was a full day, so instead of going to the inn, I sat on the back patio rocking along to the soothing sound of the ocean.

Behind me I could hear the glass door sliding open.

"My, it's such a beautiful evening. Mind if I join you?" Helen asked.

"Not at all. Here, I saved a chair for you."

"Why, thank you, my dear. I can't remember the last time I came out here in the evening and just listened to the waves. Will and I used to walk along the beach in the evening after supper. I miss those days."

I watched as she stared into the distance, remembering her past. I too was reminiscing. I thought about my time spent here with Helen and Will, about meeting the twins, and about David.

"Why do you look so downtrodden? You look as if someone broke your heart. Is it David? Did you have a bad time on your date?" she asked.

"No. It was quite the opposite. I enjoyed my time with him."

"Then why the long and sad look on your face? You have, what, an entire week of dates planned? That's something to look forward to, if it's going well," she said.

"Yeah... yeah... yeah. I know."

"What's the issue then?" she asked.

I thought long and hard about how I would articulate what I was feeling. In some ways I might be shooting myself in the foot by sharing my feelings too soon.

"Jolene? The silence is deafening. Now, clearly something is bothering you. Would you mind telling me what it is already?" She persisted.

My eyes clouded up, but I wiped them real quick. Crying wasn't something I'd usually do. Normally the brandy helped to numb all that emotional stuff.

"I'm questioning whether I'm making the right decision," I said.

"The decision to move?"

"Yes."

"Interesting. I didn't expect to hear that coming out of your mouth." She moved toward the edge of her seat, grinning from ear to ear.

"He must have done a real number on you. Did the two of you sleep together? I want to hear all the details," she said.

"Helen, why does your mind automatically go to me sleeping with David? My having second thoughts is not based on David."

"You better move out of the way before you get struck by lightning. That's what happens to people who fabricate the truth." She slapped her knee, laughing hard at her own joke, until she realized she was laughing alone.

"He might be a small part of the equation, but there's more to it than that. I may want my independence, but I don't want to be all alone, Helen. You, Will, and the girls. You're all I have. If I go back to Jacksonville, which God knows how much I love my hometown, but who's really going to look after me there? Especially when I need someone to call on. Who will be there for me? It's not like I have any children of my own to come and visit every now and again. I don't want to grow old and die alone," I said.

"Good grief, Jolene. How long has it been since you had something to drink? I almost don't recognize who you are when you're sober."

This time I was the one laughing. She was right. I did have a different personality when I wasn't drinking. For once, I was facing my feelings head on, instead of just complaining and masking my sorrows.

"Oh, Helen."

"Seriously. Who are you?" She teased before continuing.

"Listen. I'm being funny, but in all sincerity, you have to follow your gut on this one. As I said earlier, we're family, and we'll be here for you no matter the distance." Helen patted me on the knee.

"Thank you."

"Absolutely... and I'll do one better. Although we're putting feelers out there for a nurse, we still haven't found anyone yet. Maybe you would consider renting an apartment nearby so you can keep your full-time position with Will? We could even make a few revisions to include regular work hours and anything else you might need." She offered.

"Really?" I felt a weight being lifted off my shoulders.

"Yeah, sure. Why not? I'll make a deal with you. Consider trying it out for the next six months or even a year. That's the minimum time you could lease an apartment for, plus it buys us extra time to come up with a solid plan for Will, in case you still decide to leave. If it doesn't work out and you find that you still want to return to Jacksonville, then we'll all help you pack. I'll even pay for your moving truck," she said.

"You know what, Helen. I think you might have yourself a deal. This way I can really give Pelican Beach a fair shot. You know... give it the chance it really deserves. That's what David has been suggesting all along."

"Speaking of David, are you going to tell me about this date of yours or what? I guess he'll be happy to find out he has more than a week to win you over." She chuckled.

"Maybe I shouldn't say anything to him and just wait to see where the week leads me."

"Jolene, you're so bad. Don't string the guy along like that!"

"I'm only teasing, but it sure would be fun," I said.

"I'll bet."

"He's really kind, Helen. He takes his time with me... he listens to me. He's... gentle and patient. I haven't had someone like that in my life in a long time," I said.

"So, am I detecting that you're starting to have feelings for him?"

"I don't know that it's fair to assess that after one date. But, I know one thing for certain. My mind wasn't on George last night. I didn't want the evening to end. Although I've always found David to be rather easy to talk to, so I guess that's nothing new," I replied.

"I'm happy for you just the same, Jolene. You don't have to figure everything out overnight. You just have to be willing, that's all. If I think back to when you first arrived here, you've come a long way. I'm proud of you."

"Oh, boy. Here we go." I chuckled.

"I mean it. I'm not going to tell any embarrassing stories. You already know how wild and crazy you can be at times. You know I'm telling the truth."

"Yes, Helen. I know. I can't help it. It's in my blood. Us Fergusons were born crazy, what can I say?"

Helen picked up her watering can and began watering her potted plants. She fiddled around quietly for a while before returning to her chair beside me.

"Sometimes I wish I were in your shoes, Jolene."

"What do you mean?"

"Please take this the right way. I'm committed to Will till the very end. For better or for worse were the vows we exchanged, and I intend on keeping them. But, you see what our lives are like now. It's hard for him to see me the same way he used to. I miss the old Will, terribly. Everything we've been talking about has me thinking... perhaps I'm lonely, too," she said.

"Wow, I hadn't considered that. You know you can always talk to me, Helen. I'm here for you."

"Yes, I know. Most days I'm fine. You know me. I'm strong willed and determined, but it doesn't mean I don't desire to be loved."

"I understand... and that's why I believe we all need to stick together. Now more than ever. No one can ever replace the love that comes from a soulmate. I get it. But, the lesson I'm starting to learn... even though it took a while... is we were all put here on this earth to be here for one another. I'm here for you, Helen. And, I'm sorry for all the times I caused you grief up until now."

"Thank you, and I'm sorry, too. I love you, cousin," she said.

"I love you, too. Now, enough of all the sappy talk. How about we discuss those cute grandbabies of yours? Payton is a mother to twins! Can you believe it?"

That evening we spent hours outside, nurturing our bond with good conversation, over ice cream. Before going to bed, David sent me a message that said *meet me at the inn, by the beach entrance around five-thirty to watch the sunrise. You don't want to miss it. David.*

The next morning, I quietly left the house, not expecting Will and Helen to start stirring around until at least seven-thirty. It gave me plenty of time to satisfy my curiosity and sneak in a visit with David.

"Over here." He waved.

I removed my sandals and walked closer, finding David sitting on a blanket with a continental spread.

"First, I'd like to say congratulations to you. I know Payton and Cole must be thrilled the twins are finally here," he said.

"Thank you."

"Now, make yourself comfortable. I brought muffins, fruit, croissants, and there's some orange juice in the cooler. I wasn't sure what you'd like." He offered.

"You outdid yourself. To think, I almost didn't come this morning."

"Why not? Is everything okay at home?" he asked.

"Everything is fine. Knowing my luck this would be the one morning Will wakes up unusually early. I should've mentioned something to Helen about coming here this morning... I'll have to get back to the house right after sunrise."

"It won't be too long from now. Check out the gorgeous horizon over there. Isn't it magnificent?" he asked.

"It sure is. Pelican Beach has a way of captivating all of your five senses. The sound of the ocean, the breathtaking views, the feeling of digging your feet into the sand. There's nothing like it. Nothing I've ever experienced, anyway."

"Jolene."

"Yes?"

"I brought something for you."

He reached over and grabbed a seashell. It was enormous with beautiful hues of pink and beige.

"Ha, isn't that nice. As many times as I've been to the beach, I've never taken a shell home with me. This is wonderful. Thank you, David." I smiled.

"Well, there's plenty more where that came from. Maybe we need to start a small collection. That way you can decorate your place with it should you decide to stay."

"And if I don't?" I asked.

He looked back toward the sky.

"You can take it with you. This way you can have a piece of Pelican Beach nearby wherever you go," he said.

"Since when did Pelican Beach become so special to you, David? When we met, you were a traveling businessman. What happened?"

"Jolene Ferguson happened, that's what. Look, I'm not holding back the way I feel so I can sit back and watch you leave without putting up a good fight, Jolene. I think you're making a huge mistake. You have everything you need right here in Pelican Beach, with your family and with me." He argued.

"Is that so?"

"Yes, that's so. It's not easy finding the right person to fall in love and settle down with. But you, Jolene... we've developed something special that you can't deny. If there's anybody who can influence me to settle down and stop chasing the next dollar, it's you. But sometimes I honestly don't know why I bother. It seems like no matter what I say, you doubt every word of it." He mumbled.

"Well... if that's the way you feel about it, so be it. The sun is starting to rise. I guess I'll go collect a few more of these seashells for my new place here in Pelican Beach," I said, standing up and dusting off my pants.

"Wait, you're staying?"

"I am. Helen and I made an agreement that I would continue working full-time, but I'd find my own place, and keep decent hours so I can still have time for myself. I agreed to try it out for six months to a year to see how it goes," I said.

"Oh, that's great. I'm happy for you." I wasn't convinced by the sound in his voice.

David didn't have a poker face. He was wearing his feelings on his sleeve. Laying everything on the line to show me how much he cared.

"You're a terrible liar, David. I thought you'd be pleased to hear that I'm staying."

He chuckled.

"First of all, I've been called worse things, so I'll take that as a compliment. As for you staying, I really am happy. Perhaps just selfishly disappointed that I'm not part of the reason why you're staying. But, that's okay. I won't give up that easy."

"Good. I'm glad, because I don't want you to give up. I like the idea of staying here and continuing these romantic excursions with you." I smiled.

"You do?"

"Yes, I do. Now, can we take a break from all this talking for a minute. We're going to miss our opportunity to kiss while the sun is rising."

He pressed his body close to mine and made my toes curl with a soft kiss.

"Don't you worry about missing the sunrise. Now that you're staying, we can see many sunrises... together. Me and you."

"I like the way that sounds, cowboy." I teased.

"Me, too."

EPILOGUE

*M*om, Cousin Jolene, and my sisters planned a small family gathering toward the end of the summer. It was a chance for everyone to meet the twins and reconnect, and for Cousin Jolene it was a chance to reintroduce David, this time as more than a friend.

"May I have your attention, everyone." I stood next to Cole. Both of us were holding one of the babies with Emmie by our side.

"I just want to thank mom, dad, Abby, Rebecca, and Cousin Jolene from the bottom of my heart. You put together such a lovely welcome party for the twins and beautiful reunion for everyone gathered. We don't want to steal the spotlight today. We just wanted you to know from the bottom of our hearts that we are truly grateful for everything." I announced.

"Cheers to Cole and Payton, who make very beautiful babies, if I do say so myself," Jolene yelled in the background, holding up her glass to toast.

"I thought you told me she's been cutting back on the brandy now that she has a new man in her life." Rebecca's comment directed toward mom could be heard a few feet away.

"Ha, that's one-hundred percent Jolene talking. She's been on cloud nine ever since she and David made things official," Mom said.

"Made what official? What have I missed?" Cole's mother, Alice, hadn't been around to hear the latest.

"You all should be ashamed of yourselves standing over here gossiping about Cousin Jolene's business when she's only standing a few feet away," I said.

"Oh, Payton, it's good gossip. I'm sure she wouldn't mind us shouting it from the rooftop. It's official. David is here today as her man. He sold his other businesses and recently bought a house right here in Pelican Beach. Those two are getting serious. Ever since she's moved into her own place, I think they have a lot of sleepovers... or should I say, sleepless nights." Mom winked.

"Yuck. Mom, please refrain from referring to Cousin Jolene's sex life. I can't handle the mental images," Abby said.

Abby wasn't the only one who couldn't handle the mental images. Cousin Jolene, on the other hand, was just as happy and flirtatious as ever. She kind of reminded me of Blanche from the Golden girls, the way she glided around with her rouge lipstick on. The only difference was all her love and affection were directed toward David, and he soaked up every bit of it.

"Personally, I'm glad to see Jolene happy. Nobody wants to spend the rest of their life alone. She deserves love and happiness just like the rest of us. At least that's how I felt when I met my Stanley. Look at him over there having such a good time with the guys," Alice said smiling from ear to ear.

"Okay, you all are an inspiration to couples like myself and Wyatt, and Rebecca and Ethan. I mean, seriously. I feel like we need to start setting some new relationship goals," Abby said.

"You can say that again. Once I tuck my little guy in bed at night, I barely have enough energy left to take a bath, let alone turn up the heat in the bedroom." Rebecca added.

"Don't worry. You'll get there. Eventually, you'll find a groove that works for the both of you. It takes time to figure these things out. By the time you do, then you'll have to reinvent the wheel and figure each other out all over again. We're forever evolving and changing. Change is inevitable." Alice smiled.

"I agree with you, Alice. Over the years Will and I have had to change and adapt numerous times. But, they say marriage is for better or worse, right?" Mom asked.

"Yes, ma'am. That's what we said when we recited our vows, ladies. For better or for worse." Alice chimed in.

A few of our cousins from up north came over to take a picture with us. Emmie took charge of arranging the group with the adults standing in the back and the little ones up front. Afterward, we continued talking.

"Payton, I never did have a chance to ask you. How did things work out with Maxine? Did you ever get to talk with her?" Alice asked.

"We met at the shop not long before I went into labor. Alice, I don't even know where to begin. She's a vulnerable young woman, just like I was, standing at a crossroads in her life. When we spoke, it became clear that she already knew the truth about Jack. She described all the signs of a cheating, no good, low-down, dirty man. The writing was on the wall. Maybe she was just looking for confirmation of what she already knew. I'm not sure. But I do know how hard it is to leave someone, especially when you have your heart set on having a happy ending or living happily ever-after after. To make matters worse, she doesn't have anyone else to lean on. Her friends are off living their own lives and her family lives abroad." I shared.

"Oh, no. That explains a lot. She was crying out for help. She's all alone."

"I think so. But, I also believe she's fed up. If there was ever a time to discover it's time to call it quits, I'd say during the engagement would be the time," I said.

"What do you think she's going to do?"

"You know, Alice. I didn't ask. I shared my experience and tried to help as best I could without getting involved. I also drew the boundary lines and let her know that I couldn't meet with her, anymore. I wish the best for her, but you know more than anybody, family comes first."

"I agree. Good for you, Payton. You did the right thing by drawing a boundary line. I'm sure Cole agreed?" Alice asked.

"He did and now he's done with the subject and so am I. I feel like the luckiest woman alive. Cole is my best friend and soulmate, and we have three beautiful girls. What more could I ask for? Going forward, we're committed to no more drama. Just a wonderful life, filled with family, love, and happiness for the girls. That's all we really need to live a good life...wouldn't you agree?" I said.

"Yes, it was the key to many successful years of raising

Cole. If it worked for us, I know it will for you." Alice gave me a pat on the shoulder, encouraging me to continue living by that philosophy, because in the end all we truly have to rely on is love and each other.

Ready to read Beachfront Inheritance from my new Solomons Island series? Check out the "Also By" section to learn more.

Beachfront Inheritance: Book One

She's single, out of a job, and has a week to decide what to do with her life.

Clara's boss, Joan Russell, was a wealthy owner of a beachfront mansion, who recently passed away. Joan's estranged family members have stepped in, eager to collect their inheritance and dismiss Clara of her duties.

Clara dedicated the last ten years of her life to serving Mrs. Russell as her housekeeper and dear friend. Her services are terminated, and it's now time for her to start life over again. As she prepares to move out of her living quarters, there are many thoughts to consider. What will she do with her career? Where will she live? Clara knew she would have to face these questions eventually, but she didn't expect her time with Mrs. Russell to come to such an abrupt end.

With the clock winding down, will Clara find a job and make a new life for herself on Solomons Island? Will she ever settle down and have an opportunity at love again? Or will Clara have to do the unthinkable and return home to a family who barely cares for her existence?

Embark on a journey of new beginnings and pick up your copy today!